THE CORPSE THAT SPOKE

by ROBERT H. LEITFRED

WILDSIDE PRESS

TO
WALLY AND GILMORE
TWO GRAND DICKS

1

WITHIN THE WEB

TRAILING a long streamer announcing the opening of a new chain drugstore, a fat blimp chugged across the hot sky above the coastal city. Down below the pavements fried pleasantly beneath a benevolent sun. Listless shoppers crowded the sidewalks and stores, all of them unaware of the blimp and its fluttering streamer.

People from the East called this Pacific coast city an upstart that was striving desperately to be metropolitan. Perhaps it was for there was fabulous wealth all around its far-flung boundaries. Gold at its county line; oil wells—acres of them to the north, south and east. There were also citrus groves, talkies, politics, horse-racing, and rackets by the score.

In this city, nationalists lived together with equanimity and poise. The Chinese held their tong wars like gentlemen, ate rice and were peaceful. The Japanese minded their own business, held colorful ceremonies, ate rice, and fished the waters of the Pacific with a skill that disconcerted the wily Portuguese. And the Mexicans kept goats, and the peace, content with tortillas, beans and mañana.

But there were other citizens who were not so peaceful. They moved about in devious ways above and below the fringe of the underworld. They took their toll from the honest and dishonest alike.

Mark Schilling was a citizen who lived on both levels. From ward healer, councilman and supervisor, he had climbed the political ladder. And having reached a high point, he resigned from the city payroll for the more lucrative field of a political boss—with notable success.

His office was located on the fifth floor of the Commerce building, facing the street. The frosted glass on the door was ambiguously scribed in chaste letters: MARK SCHILLING, CONSULTANT.

3

A remarkable feature of his office was not generally known to the public. It was entirely surrounded by other offices. It was possible, after leaving the elevator, to enter any of these offices and pass into Mark Schilling's inner office. But it was impossible to do so without first being scrutinized through an ingenious periscopic arrangement watched over by a sallow-faced man behind a door of an importer's office.

Being a small city boss, and without ideas of his own, Mark Schilling had copied certain features from his betters in Chicago and New York, and equipped his office with melodramatic features more showy than useful. In this respect he typified the coastal city that was striving desperately to be metropolitan.

The web-like structure of these offices, and the innumerable threads that spread out from them were not apparent at first glance. Beside a switchboard operated by a platinum blonde whose mouth was like a steel trap, there were three private lines not listed in the telephone directory.

One connected with a certain office in the City Hall. A second ended in Schilling's apartment farther uptown. And the third led to a private room in a gambling club.

And in the center of this web, like a voluptuous spider, sat Mark Schilling—a gross figure with a cherubic face cradled on three chins.

There was nothing hard in Schilling's face. No suggestion of Satan-like qualities in his pale, blue eyes. His lips were thick, his cheeks were pink with good living. And his pudgy hands, dimpled at the knuckles, seemed incapable of any form of violence.

They quickened into action as a buzzer sounded beneath his desk. "Hello," he said, lifting the receiver from the hook. "Yeah. I've been trying to get you for an hour. What's holding up that gravel contract? Well, you'd better find out. No, I'm not threatening you. I'm just telling you. Okay."

He returned the instrument to the hook and struck a match to a cigar. Again the buzzer vibrated beneath the desk. His pale, blue eyes were void of expression as he listened. "I've fixed it with the Parole Board," he said. "Your friend will be on the streets in a couple days."

He closed the connection and held the hook down with pudgy fingers. He lifted them after a moment. "Marie," he said to the operator with the steel-trap mouth. "Get me the Chromium Novelty Company. I want the manager, Herman Yates."

A voice came over the wire after a time. "Chromium Novelty."

"Mr. Yates?" asked Schilling. "About those slot machines with which your company is flooding the city. They're nice machines, Yates. Beautiful in fact. But on the mechanical side there's a lot to be desired for the saps that put out nickels to play them. Do you get my point, Yates?"

"Not exactly, no."

"It comes to this, Yates. The percentage in your favor is too great. It amounts to gambling. The city won't stand for it. Our inspectors have checked them thoroughly. The chance for winning on them is less than two per cent. You'll have to take them out."

"Wait a second," said Yates. "Maybe this can be fixed."

"Fixed?" Schilling raised an eyebrow.

"Say a cut of fifteen percent on the gross take . . ."

"Twenty-five," corrected Schilling. "These things are difficult to handle. Twenty-five percent of the gross earnings on every machine in town. We have a record of every one that has been installed. I'll send a man to your office to collect. You can pay him. In cash."

"Okay," said Yates. "But who are you? And how will I be sure that the cops won't . . ."

"You'll be left alone," said Schilling, "as long as you pay out that twenty-five percent. Take it or leave it."

"I'll take it,"said Yates. "Send over your man."

Mark Schilling grunted as he got to his feet. Ponderously he waddled to the windows facing Broadway. His pale blue eyes watched the surging crowds. He took the cigar from between his teeth. It was a good cigar.

He knocked the ashes into a brass tray. Not only was the cigar good, but everything was good. His rackets were good. Good? They were perfect. He had money in five different banks, cached in safety deposit boxes. No tracing him with ledger accounts.

Yes, everything was good. Even repeal hadn't cut in on his income. He almost had the city in the palm of his hand. Give him time. A couple more years. The weakening of his machine a year ago when the District Attorney had been indicted and sent to the state penitentiary for a number of years had almost worn out. True, a number of his judges had resigned from the bench at the request of an aroused citizenry.

That, too, would soon be completely remedied. After all, Judges were human. If they proved stubborn, it was not impossible to dig up something out of their past—something they generally had forgotten.

And if there had been no past, that, too, could be remedied. Mark Schilling had reason to be proud of himself and his organization which functioned with the smoothness of a well-oiled machine. He had reason to be proud of the safeguards with which he had surrounded himself.

Granting someone should squeal, which was always possible in any set-up, there would always be the fall guy to take the rap. He, himself, was untouchable. He paid his men well for their loyalty. Repaid them equally well for carelessness or treachery. In this respect he was without a shred of pity or conscience. And he never allowed himself to trust anyone—completely.

A light flickered from the ceiling which meant that someone was coming into the inner office by way of the contractor's office. Mark Schilling waddled back to his chair and pressed a button flush with the mahogany desk top but concealed by a blotter.

A short, thick-set man entered through a section of wall panel that noiselessly opened. After he entered, it closed behind him. The man was known as Gat O'Brien. But, he never carried a gat unless he knew he was going to use it. Those were his instructions. Schilling never kept a man long on his payroll who refused to obey orders. Three of this type had already found themselves keeping company with the former district attorney behind gray walls.

Mark Schilling's cherubic face was faintly questioning as he nodded to his henchman. "What's on your mind, Gat?"

"I just come," said O'Brien, "from Judge Chadwick's court. Geez, there was a lot of palaver going on over there." He helped himself to an imported cigar from the box on Schilling's desk. "You sure know how to pick 'em, Boss. Best cigars . . ."

"And what did you hear in Chadwick's court?"

"Larkin's bail has been set at fifty grand. It looks bad for that guy. It sure does. If he wasn't guilty as hell, I'd say that the D. A. was making a grandstand play with a handful of bum cards. It looks bad. It looks like they had something on Larkin after all—especially the judge."

"Fifty grand," repeated Schilling. "Is Chadwick crazy?"

"No," said O'Brien, shaking his head. "Not him. He's what I call a hard, tough baby. He's got ideas, that old buzzard has. Well, it looks like Larkin won't jump his bail bond and fade into the Styx until this business blows over. It looks like he'd have to face the rap."

"You wouldn't have any idea, Gat," said Schilling, quietly, "what caused Judge Chadwick to place the bond so high?"

"Who, me? Say, you kidding me, Boss?"

"Not now. This is too serious. That bail shouldn't have been a nickel more than ten grand when you figure how little the D. A. has in the way of evidence."

"That's what I thought. That's why I come to see you soon as I saw how things were stacking up against Larkin."

"Fifty thousand dollars," muttered Schilling, rubbing his fat hands together. "It looks, Gat, as though something will have to be done. It'll be tough on Nickey if the dicks begin sweating Larkin and he starts to talk."

The face of Gat O'Brien twitched slightly. "So I figured. You want me to turn on the heat? I don't like judges. Never did."

Schilling's eyebrow moved upward. "Heat?" He shook his big head. The rolls of fat beneath his jaws quivered like waves of jelly. "Nothing so crude as the heat treatment, Gat. That's for men who haven't brains with which to reason. Putting judges on the spot is bad business."

"Sure. I get what you mean. But that ain't helping Larkin any."

"No," agreed Mark Schilling. "It ain't helping Larkin any. Something will have to be done."

He saw out of the corner of his eye the warning flicker from the ceiling—a double flash. Which meant that someone was waiting to see him via the office of the dentist.

It was a cardinal principle of Mark Schilling's that the less his henchmen know of each other, the less chance there was of things going wrong. O'Brien had entered the office through the contractor's rooms. He never came any other way. In fact he knew nothing of the secret doors leading to the dentist and the importer's suites.

"What do you think I ought to do?" asked O'Brien.

"Nothing," said Schilling. "Keep out of sight for a few days till I get the Larkin business lined up. When I'm ready, I'll let you know."

"Okay!" Gat O'Brien nodded, swung on his heel and went through the swinging panel of the wall.

When it had closed, the fat man took a leather-bound memorandum book from his pocket. In it was a list of names. He studied them for a time, sighed, and with a pencil drew a heavy line through an entry reading:

Biff Larkin. National City Bank hold-up. Witnesses, cashier and taxi driver. Comments: Too much popular feeling.

He returned the book to his pocket. Larkin was finished. Mark Schilling was washing his hands of the man. He hadn't the slightest intention of paying out this huge amount. The price was too high. Larkin, having jumped his bond, would have to go into hiding. Of what use would such a man be to the organization? None at all.

Had the case been scheduled for any other court than Chadwick's, Mark Schilling would have been in no hurry to draw a line through Larkin's name. As it was there was nothing he could do. In all things Mark Schilling was ruthless. His success, so far, lay in playing safe.

He pressed a second button beneath the blotter on his desk. Another section of wall panel swung inward. Through it came Police Lieutenant Michael Bemus in civilian clothes.

"How are you, Mike," beamed Schilling. "Just the man I wanted to see."

"Yeah?" said Bemus, relaxing heavily into a chair. "What's on your mind, Mark. I haven't much time. Got to be back on duty in an hour."

Schilling nodded heavily. "How'd you come out on the races at Santa Anita?"

"The bookies took me to the cleaners. Your hot tip was cold. I dropped five hundred smackers on the race you said was fixed."

Mark Schilling looked hurt, crestfallen. "Now that's too bad, Mike. Just too bad. I don't like my friends to be treated like that." He took a thick wad of money from his pocket and counted off five notes. "Here," he said. "Five centuries. Try it again sometime. I can't be a hundred percent right. But I hold a pretty good average."

"Thanks, Mark," said Bemus, pocketing the money. "By the way, is there anything new on my getting the Captaincy of the Eleventh Precinct?"

Mark Schilling leaned back in the swivel chair and crossed his pudgy hands on his paunch. "Now don't you worry, Mike. Things are a little slow right now. But I haven't forgotten the promise I made to you. Leave everything to me. I promised you the job, and I'll see that you get the appointment."

Through half-closed eyes he studied the police officer. "Bemus," he said, in a voice of a different tone, "just what has the D. A. got on this guy Larkin? I heard that Judge Chadwick has set his bail at fifty grand. That's a lot of money. They must be pretty sure they can convict."

"Convict?" said Bemus, twisting his lips into something meant for a smile. "Captain Jorgens has got that guy on ice, Mark. But it isn't Larkin who means so much to the National City. He got away with a nice wad—thirty-five thousand smackers. We know because we recovered the loot in his rooming house."

Mark Schilling's eyes were almost closed. He seemed half asleep. "It's all very interesting, Bemus. But you were saying . . ."

The grimace intended for a smile on the police officer's face turned into a scowl. "It's like this, Mark. The National City reported a loss of two-hundred thousand dollars. All that Larkin got away with was a measly thirty-five. Get the fine point? That hold-up was planned from within—by someone who rates big in the institution. In other words it was a cover-up job."

"And Larkin," resumed Schilling, "is nothing . . ."

"Nothing but a fall guy," said Bemus.

Mark Schilling said nothing. But he was thinking swiftly. Only a few days before the bank stick-up, its cashier had been in this office with him trying to arrange a loan that would see him through the next visit of the bank examiner.

Schilling had turned the cashier down. Refused. And then, when the hold-up had taken place a few days later, the cashier must have pulled a fast one. He had raised the loss from thirty-five to two hundred thousand—enough to wipe out his defalcation, and have plenty of gravy left over.

"You look," said Bemus, "like a cat that has just lapped up a saucer of cream."

"Funny," said Mark Schilling, visualizing this new source of revenue to be tapped when he put pressure on this crooked cashier, "but that's just the way I feel."

2

OUTSIDE THE WEB

ON THE seventh floor of a building not a great distance from the Commerce structure where Mark Schilling manipulated the strings of his various puppets, another man had his suite of offices.

Compared with those of Schilling, they were small and meagre. There were no secret panels in the walls, no imported cigars on the desk, no system of lights announcing visitors, and no lookout watching the hallway and elevators.

The glass panel of the door was labeled: SIMON CROLE, SPECIAL INVESTIGATOR. In the reception room as one entered Crole's office was the secretary's desk. And behind it sat Etta, plump, bland and keen. To the right and left of her desk were two doors. One led to a cubby-hole of a room generally used by Crole's operator, Matt Ridley. It was Ridley's practice, when not out a case, to sit close to a thin partition and listen to the wails and laments of the many clients seeking the private detective's aid.

The other door, near Etta's desk, led directly to Simon Crole's inner office. In it were chairs, a wardrobe, a leather-covered sofa, and a scarred desk. This desk was used principally for Crole's feet, and a place on which to lean.

He sat behind it now, his feet resting comfortably on its

scarred surface. He was a big man, but not as big as Schilling.
And there was a certain feline grace in his every movement.
He was bald. Fanwise wrinkles slanted outwards from the corners of his eyes. His lips were slightly askew from an ancient
scar, creating the illusion, and falsely, that the private detective
was in a state of perpetual surprise. All of which was far from
the truth.

Nearly a week had passed since Mark Schilling had crossed
the name of Larkin from the pages of his leather-bound book.
Since the district attorney and his assistants had all the evidence
necessary to convict, and since the tide of popular feeling was
running high, the trial had been scheduled to take place in
Judge Chadwick's court, and was well under way. When no
capable criminal lawyer came forward to defend Larkin, the
Court had appointed a defense attorney. This was unusual, for
men like Larkin generally had their own lawyers.

But no one noticed this, except, perhaps, a few of Larkin's associates. District Attorney Minifie was grimly efficient as he
moved about among his assistants. Captain Jorgens, and the
police sergeant who had made the arrest, were present along
with the witnesses of which there were none for the defense.
Their faces were grave with a duty well done.

Simon Crole, his feet still on the desk, had read part of this
in the paper, and had surmised the rest. To him it seemed
commonplace enough. The only unusual feature, he thought,
was the fact that the cashier had so much money in his cage.
He wondered, also, why the police were so slow in grabbing
Larkin's accomplice. Routine stuff.

The daylight holdup of the National City was an accomplished fact. It should have ended then and there. But what
Simon Crole didn't know was this: If Larkin and his accomplice had succeeded, the fat man in the Commerce building
would have received as his share, a substantial part of the loot.
The fact that Larkin had been nabbed, and part of the money
recovered, altered things entirely.

Mark Schilling had no intention of revealing his hand in
the affair if there was nothing to be gained by it. The case was
too hot. He didn't care to burn his fingers. Larkin was little
better than a punk. And punks were easily replaced.

Yet the Larkin case was not to end with the arrest and conviction of this one man. An irresistible force had been set in motion which no one man could forsee—much less, control.

It had already started to gather momentum. For at that moment, while Simon Crole was thrusting the Larkin case from his mind as routine stuff, a close friend of the bank robber, who, strangely enough, was an honest man having no connection with Larkin's criminal activities, was entering the front office.

He stood, at this very moment, just inside the frosted panel door, his cap in his hand, facing the secretary.

Etta eyed him blandly. "Something?" she asked.

"Yeah," said the man. "I want to talk to the boss."

"Mr. Crole is busy just now. Anything I can do?"

"I don't want to talk to no jane," said the man. "I want to talk with Mr. Crole. No, it ain't about myself. It's about a friend of mine who's in trouble. I don't know as Mr. Crole can do anything about it, but I got to talk to him so's to find out. When can I see him?"

"Have a chair," said Etta, smilingly. "And who, did you say, was your friend?"

"I didn't say, sister. His name is Biff Larkin."

"Oh!" Etta reached for the extension phone. "A man outside to see you," she said to her invisible listener, "about the Larkin affair. Interested?"

"Does he look," came Crole's deep voice from the receiver, "like he had lots of dough?"

"No."

"Get rid of him then. We've been stuck with too many clients who can't pay their bills."

"I'm sorry," said Etta, no longer smiling. "But Mr. Crole is rather busy just now. And I don't think he'd be interested in your friend Larkin."

The man in the outer office rose slowly from the chair. His slow smile failed to conceal the disappointment in his eyes. They stared dumbly at the cap clutched in his grimy fingers. "Sorry, sister," he said. "I didn't think I had much of a chance, but you can't blame a guy for trying."

His hand was reaching for the knob of the door when the buzzer sounded beneath the secretary's desk. Etta took the receiver from the hook, listened, smiled and hung up. "Mr. Crole will see you after all," she said. She indicated with a well-manicured hand the door beside her desk. "Walk right in," she said.

Simon Crole had removed his feet from the desk and was fumbling with a cloth sack of tobacco when the man entered. "Hello," he said. "What's on your mind?"

"My name's King," said the man. "I work at the central garage on Third street. I'm a friend of Biff Larkin, but I ain't no crook, believe it or not."

"Ummm!" grunted the private detective, finishing his cigarette and lighting it with a trick lighter. He regarded his visitor critically. "A friend of Larkin, eh? It isn't good business, King, to admit something like this—especially right now when the police are checking Larkin's friends and associates."

"Sure. I ain't so dumb as not to know that. But the fact is, me and Larkin were pals before he went haywire and got to runnin' around with a cheap bunch of crooks. He didn't have no trade like me, so when the depression comes he couldn't get a job."

"So he turns to robbin' banks and gets caught," added Crole.

"Yeah. But I ain't holdin' it against him. Biff knew the chances he was takin'. And when the cops gather him over in his roomin' house he don't make a squawk. He's guilty as hell and he knows it."

"Just what," asked Crole, inhaling deeply, "do you expect me to do, if anything."

"I'm gettin' to that point," said King. "Just before the cops pinch him he comes over to where I work and backs me into a corner. 'King,' he says, 'I got to lam out of town. Me and another guy just nicked the National City for thirty-five grand. I'll be seein' you when the storm blows over. If you need any jack, all you gotta do is say so. I'm lousy with it.' Then he blows over to his roomin' house."

"He didn't," asked Crole, "tell you who this other guy was, did he?"

"Sure. A wop by the name of Nicky Lombardo."

"And who," asked Crole, casually, "is Nicky Lombardo?"

"I dunno," said King. "That's just a name I heard Biff use."

"I see," said Crole.

"No, you don't see yet," said King. "I ain't finished. There's that little matter of what Larkin actually got from the bank, and what the papers printed that he stole. The police seemed to have overlooked that part. I know Biff got only thirty-five grand. He told me. And he ain't got no reason for lyin'."

"You figure someone else besides Larkin copped the difference?"

"Yeah, that's why I'm here. I could have gone to the police. But hell, I can't tell them I'm a friend of Larkin's. Where would it get me?"

"Your point, if you have one," said Crole, examining the hot end of his cigarette, "still eludes me."

"It's like this, Mr. Crole. When Biff rests the chopper he's carryin' on the bank window, the cashier looks up. His face turns white, and he starts pushin' money under the grille. Then all of a sudden he starts to grin. That grin makes Biff nervous. He thinks for a moment someone is behind him, but he didn't turn around. He just shoved the stuff in his pocket and beat it. But he didn't forget how that cashier grinned."

Crole said, without a change of expression, "It looks like that cashier thought of something pleasant—so pleasant in fact that it made him forget his immediate danger from the chopper."

"That's correct, Mr. Crole. That's all I got to tell you. I thought somebody ought to know this. Not that it will help Larkin. He's stuck right now. But I don't like the idea of someone usin' him as a lever to pry a hundred and sixty-five grand from the depositors of the National City."

"Then you're not here to hire me to work for Larkin?"

"Hell no. I ain't got no money. I just come here to tip you off. If that lousy cashier is guilty of liftin' the bank's money, I don't see no reason why he shouldn't be in the same place Biff's headed for."

He got to his feet. "I guess that's all, Mr. Crole. I've heard you were the best private detective in this town. So I guess you'll know what to do about this information."

"I guess I will," lied the private detective. "Thanks for coming in, King. I don't know but what it might be best to get in touch with the police. Withholding information you know."

"Well, I got it out of *my* system. Do as you please. But I'm glad I told somebody."

Simon Crole watched the man go without getting up from

his chair. His eyes were thoughtful. He rubbed his nose. The cashier had smiled when he shoved thirty-five thousand dollars beneath the grille. He had smiled when there was no reason for smiling—or was there?

He stopped rubbing his nose. His eyes grew more thoughtful. He turned the information over in his mind, tested it from all angles, and tried to estimate its financial worth from a personal standpoint. But Simon Crole, whatever his faults, and they were many, was no blackmailer.

Yet, when a piece of information was dropped into his lap, it was not his policy to immediately turn it over to the police unless he received more than he gave.

Having no favors to ask of the police, he decided it might be to his advantage to squeeze this particular item of information dry before turning it over to Police Captain Jorgens to worry about.

He knew beyond a shadow of doubt that the police had not overlooked the cashier. Nor had the district attorney and his nimble assistants. But none of them had seen the cashier smile. So that would seem to be that. And yet . . .

The fanwise wrinkles slanting outward from the corners of his eyes deepened as he considered the angle of Larkin's accomplice in the bank hold-up. Now who the devil was Nicky Lombardo? He might find out through an examination of police records—that is, if Lombardo had a record on file.

The buzzer beneath his desk broke in on his speculations. He listened to Etta's honeyed voice announcing a wealthy client in the outer office.

"Send her in, precious," he purred into the mouthpiece, putting the Larkin case from his mind.

The client came in. She was a tall, angular woman, with her hair wadded on top of her head, and crowned with a picture hat, vintage of two generations past. Her mouth was large, and opened to the weather, displaying two rows of perfect porcelain.

She came through the door clicking them like castanets. Evidently she was considerably worked up.

"How do you do," she said, briskly. "You're Simon Crole, I take it?"

Crole offered her a chair. "I'm Simon Crole, Madame."

"Well, I must say you don't look like a private detective. You look like a Chinese Buddha. But that's neither here nor there, Mr. Crole. I'm a woman of few words, but those words are always decisive. Do you know anything about following people? You should, God knows. That's your business."

"I'm an excellent follower," stated Crole, with just the right amount of modesty.

"You are? Very well. Then you could, without any difficulty, follow my husband if necessary, and report on his movements from day to day."

"Mere routine, Madame. And who is your husband?"

The porcelains clicked a lively tune as the lady fumbled in her reticule for a card. Crole had no scruples against looking into the open bag. He saw, with a pleasurable glow, that it was stuffed with bills. Etta had gauged the client with unerring skill.

"There it is," announced the lady, laying a card on the private detective's desk. "And here is a picture taken only a few weeks ago."

Simon Crole examined the card. On it was printed: August Fweeble. Below the printing in angular handwriting was the name and address of an apartment. He next examined the picture. The snapshot revealed a jaunty little man with twinkling eyes, knicker suit, plaid golf hose, and a wide, mobile mouth. Evidently a sport and a rare one, thought the private detective.

"Good character in your husband's face," he approved, unconsciously falling into error.

"Character?" Mrs. Fweeble's eyes gave off sparks. The double row of porcelains clicked storm warnings. "Character?" she repeated. "Perhaps. But it's very slight. Very. He's an old fool. He's in his dotage. He drinks to excess. He gambles. And . . ." her lips compressed themselves into a tight knot. "And he may have a mistress."

Simon Crole shook his head sadly. "That's unfortunate, Mrs. Fweeble. A case like this requires delicate handling. However, I can do it. I can have your husband followed, his every movement traced, and give you a complete report at the end of every day he is under my surveillance."

Mrs. Fweeble nodded energetically. "Good. Very good. And your rates for this surveillance, as you call it, are . . ."

"My fee for this type of work is a flat one hundred and fifty a day, Madame, plus any additional expenses my operators may encounter aside from meals and taxi fares. Two days' fee in advance is the usual practice, Madame."

Mrs. Fweeble opened her reticule a second time, counted out a stack of twenty and ten dollar bills and placed them on the scarred desk. "There," she stated, grimly. "When will you start?"

Crole eyed the money but made no move to touch it. "Shall we say tomorrow morning, Madame?"

"No. You will begin your surveillance tonight. My husband sleeps most of the day, and like a tomcat, starts his prowls with the coming of darkness."

Crole nodded. "Just as you say. I'll have an operator in front of your apartment at about seven. He'll pick up Mr. Fweeble as he leaves and he'll remain somewhere near him till he returns home. Tomorrow my secretary will mail you your first report."

"Good. Very good." Mrs. Fweeble rose to her feet, gathered her reticule beneath her arm, adjusted her hat, which didn't need adjusting, and again drew her lips into a tight knot. "Can you imagine a man carrying on the way he does at his age?" Her eyes snapped. From the door leading to the outer office she turned. "The old fool!" she flung at Crole.

A tremendous sigh whistled from the private detective's lips after the old lady had left. He scooped the bills from the desk. Counted them, shoved two of the twenties into his pocket and took the rest to his secretary.

"Bank it, precious," he instructed her. "And open an account with Mrs. August Fweeble. Advance fee, three hundred dollars. And charge my personal account with forty dollars. Then see if you can get Esther on the wire."

He returned to his desk and sat down. After a moment the phone rang. Crole took down the receiver. "Social Welfare headquarters," said a pleasant voice.

Crole said: "Don't be high-hat with Simon, Esther darling."

"Old dear," came Esther's voice. "Please be brief."

"A Mr. August Fweeble. Wealthy, a sport, and in his dotage. He steps out every night. I'm to find out where and why. I pick him up tonight at his home. Care to come along?"

"Old men in their dotage don't sound very interesting."

. "This one will. He goes places. He does things. Be ready at seven. I'll pick you up in a taxi."

At precisely seven o'clock, Esther Manning, in a vermilion evening dress and cape, came down the stairs of her home to the taxi waiting at the curb. She was tall, slender, and strikingly beautiful. From a clever store detective she had graduated to Crole's office as an operator. After being with him two years she had further graduated into police work, and finally into social service. Nights she had studied law, and had just passed the bar examination. Her goal was the bench, with criminal law as a stepping-stone.

"You're beautiful," said Crole, as he held open the taxi door.

"And thirsty, too, old dear. Likewise, I'm starved."

"Both will soon be corrected." He gave an address to the driver and the cab moved away from the curb to stop after a time across the street from the Fweeble home.

They didn't wait long. A jaunty, light-stepping gentleman in evening clothes came out of the side door of the apartment house and got into a rakish roadster. As it swerved from the drive, Crole's taxi fell in behind.

The lights of the city were on, and darkness had fallen when the roadster turned into the gravel drive of the Green Gate, a famous roadhouse.

"Well," observed Crole, as the taxi slowed to a stop where the gravel drive ended at the state highway, "here we are. Gus can sure pick swell places. This place is notorious for sidecars and chicken . . ." He stopped abruptly.

Thinly through the night came the brittle crackling of gunfire. A man screamed chokingly. Crole looked at his companion. She returned his stare saying drily: "A swell place you've brought me to. Was this shooting down on the cards?"

. "No," said Simon Crole, opening the taxi door. "It wasn't." He started up the drive on the run, checked himself and ducked back into the shrubbery bordering the drive.

As he did so a small coupe, without lights, swerved down the drive, grazed a tree with its right rear fender, and went skirling down the highway citywards.

Simon Crole stepped out of the shrubbery. He saw a man with a flashlight moving towards the shadows of a far corner of the bricked courtyard where a few cars were parked. The beam of light played momentarily over the rear end of a police motorcycle revealing an oblong metal plate. The license number was X-309.

Crole hurried and caught up with the man carrying the flash. "What's happened?" he puffed.

"How should I know. I heard the sound of guns as I drove in. A car swerved out of the parking line. It didn't look good to me, so I thought I'd look things over."

"Give me the flash," ordered Crole. He kept on walking forward. And then he stopped. Held out his arm to check the other man, and began to swear softly.

Two men lay on the bricked surface of the parking lot. One of them wore the uniform of the State police. Crole bent over him. The officer was dead. He turned his attention to the other victim, a flashily dressed man with a swarthy skin. The man was moaning with pain.

"Keep back," ordered Crole, to his companion. He bent down over the wounded man. "Hurt bad?" he asked.

"Get Mark," husked the wounded man in a voice so low that only the crouching agency man could hear. "Tell him it's Nick . . . tell him it's Nicky Lom . . ." Froth, bright red, bubbled from the man's lips. He breathed harshly and with great effort.

"What did he say?" asked the man with the flashlight.

"I couldn't hear him," said Crole, deliberately lying. He straightened and flung a curious glance at his companion. The man, he discovered, now that his eyes were accustomed to the gloom of the courtyard, was August Fweeble. "We'd better go inside, Mister," he continued, "and call an ambulance and the police."

As Fweeble trotted on ahead, Simon Crole turned to Esther only a few feet away. "Murder," he told her bluntly. "A motor cop. Also, and this is important in a way, to me, a man by the name of Nicky Lombardo was badly wounded. The third man got away."

Esther Manning gripped his arm. "Are you mixed up in this, Simon?"

He shook his head. "Not yet, girl. But I've got a feeling that

I'm going to be, whether I want to or not. At any rate, I'm due for a grilling from the police as soon as they arrive."

3

GENTLEMEN'S AGREEMENT

THE grilling, as Simon Crole had anticipated, was well under way. Police Captain Jorgens, his teeth clamped aggressively on an unlighted cigar, sat at their table in a private alcove. His knuckles showed white from gripping the table's edge.

Next to Crole sat Esther, inscrutible as a Sphinx, her fingers entwined around the stem of the frosted glass containing the sidecar. Across from her sat August Fweeble, his twinkling eyes wide with pleasurable excitement, a bottle of Bourbon within easy reach, and a half empty glass beside it.

"I want to get this straight," Jorgens was saying. "Exactly what happened when your taxi stopped out on the highway?"

"I opened the door," said Crole. "I got out. Then I heard the sound of guns. And I thought to myself, someone's gonna get hurt."

"Never mind what you thought. What did you do then?"

"I went up the drive. Heard the roar of a motor as a car without lights came tearing down the drive. Ducked into the shrubbery to keep from getting run over; saw the car, a coupe, swing onto the state highway. Then I continued up the drive the way I started. I met this gentleman on the way."

"That's right," broke in Fweeble. "I had a flashlight. Always carry one in my car. My wife's forever losing her hairpins . . ."

"Pretty old guy, aren't you," quizzed the police officer, facing Fweeble, "to be hanging about a joint like this?"

"I'm old, Captain. That's a fact." Fweeble chuckled pleasantly. "But I got young ideas."

Jorgens faced Crole again. "You were saying, Simon . . ."

"This man had the flashlight," resumed Crole. "Together we walked over to the corner section of the parking lot. There we found the bodies. I looks at the cop and figures he's dead. Then I bent over the other man. He's alive. He moans something which isn't clear."

"Maybe it wasn't clear to you. Exactly what did he say?"

"I couldn't make it out."

"Oh, hell, why are you lying? You must have heard something. At least a word or two."

"I heard words all right," said Crole, unperturbed. "But they didn't make sense. Sorta like gurgles."

"Did your friend," nodding towards Esther, "did she hear . . "

Esther's scarlet lips savored the sidecar. "No, fortunately. I was some distance from where the bodies were found."

The police officer took the cigar from between his lips, examined its chewed end, frownd, and shook his grizzled head slowly. "Simon," he said, "get this straight. A motor cop was shot to death. No reason, apparently. Just bumped off, wantonly. And another man critically wounded. No gun to be found anywheres. A third man gets away. The boys at the different station houses are going to be sore. They don't kill cops in this town and get away with it."

Crole rubbed his bald head. "Right, Jorgens."

"Well, we're going after that guy that lammed out in the coupe. We'll get him, too. And remember this, Simon. If you're directly or indirectly mixed up in this shooting, your toes are going to get trampled on. The D. A. will be wanting to see you anyway. Maybe you'll talk to him when you wouldn't to me."

Simon Crole blinked stupidly. "I'm hungry, Captain, and so are my friends. So don't expect me to cry over your troubles. I got plenty of my own. Have a drink before you close the inquisition?"

"Keep your drinks," stormed the captain, rising to his feet. "And remember this, Simon. If your hands are dirty, don't blame me if the boys get rough with you." Still frowning, he barged from the alcove into the main dining room.

"Nice police officer," sighed Esther. "So refined."

"I think I'll be going," suggested Fweeble.

"Stick around," said Crole. "I kinda like you. So does Esther."

The girl's smile went to work on the old man. "I like the way you talked to that policeman, Mr. Fweeble. You were splendid."

Fweeble squared his narrow shoulders. "I wish my wife could hear you say that. I certainly do. She thinks I'm a worm —a sly, old worm."

"Fweeble," said Crole, "are you a good mixer?"

"I'm fair."

"Do your stuff. Here comes the waiter with a trayful of bottles. And behind him comes another with our dinner. Work fast, old boy, and I'll tell you a nice story when the dishes are cleared away."

The dishes, eventually, were cleared away. Crole, studying the amber fluid in his glass, said: "Fweeble, what's your game?"

"Game?" The man's twinkling eyes were suddenly alert.

"You're an older man than I am," resumed the private detective, "And, like that police officer remarked, too old for this sort of thing."

"You aren't," said Fweeble, setting down an empty glass, "going to spoil all this by lecturing an old man, are you?"

"I remarked, Fweeble, that I was . . ."

"Call me Gus."

"As I started to say, Gus," went on Crole, blandly, "I was going to tell you a nice story."

"Don't delay too long, Mr. Crole. The dance orchestra starts in a few minutes."

"Plenty of time," said Crole. "How about another drink."

"Make mine a sidecar," said Esther, throwing another dazzling smile on the jaunty, little man across the table. "We want to hear that nice story, don't we Gus?"

Fweeble beamed. "Of course. I'm very much interested in Mr. Crole. He's so direct." Deftly he mixed drinks and passed them around.

"Gus," said Crole, "I like you. So does Esther."

"Sounds like a touch," chuckled Fweeble. "I seem to detect a certain familiar technique."

Simon Crole's lips pursed in a smile. He seemed surprised, which he was not. It occurred to him that this jaunty, little man had been around in the course of his life.

"Gus," he continued, "do you know what my business is?"

Fweeble smacked his lips after a short drink. "You are," he said, "either a politician, a lawyer or . . ."

"Or what?"

"The last evades me. Not quite clear in my mind. What are you?"

"A private detective."

Fweeble nodded. "That's it. You specialize in scandal, divorce and all the odds and ends the police leave around loose."

"I specialize mostly in crime, Gus. I don't care much for the odds and ends, that's why I'm talking to you this way. Now listen. I'll be frank with you."

"I hope so."

"Here's the dope. I've been retained to follow you and report everything you do, and everywhere you go to your wife. Until such time as you are no longer under my surveillance, or that of my operators, you can't do a single thing that won't be reported to her. For this work I am paid well. It's mere routine for my agency."

Something seemed to happen to Gus Fweeble. His shoulders sagged. The gay look left his eyes. He pushed his drink away. He looked extremely unhappy.

"I'm sorry to hear about this. Hannibal shouldn't have done it."

"Maybe not, Gus, but she's afraid, among other things, that you have a mistress."

A flicker of a smile returned to the old fellow's face, and vanished as quickly as it had come. "Hannibal's been reading too many romance novels lately. No, it's nothing like that. I've worked hard all my life and made a lot of money. But I never had any fun. I don't ask much—just silly things mostly that I don't get at home."

He pushed his glass even farther away as if it offended him.

"Don't be that way," said Crole. "There's a way out."

"But there won't be any fun in life," complained Fweeble, "with you and your disguised operators following me about. The charm of going around, where I wanted to go, and doing what I wanted, will be gone." He eyed his drink with vast melancholy.

"Finish your drink," invited Crole, genially, "and I'll continue where I left off."

"You might as well stop. I've heard enough."

"Let me tell you something, Gus. Your wife hired me. She pays me with your money. Is there any reason, aside from an ethical one, why you shouldn't hire me too?"

August Fweeble allowed this to sink in. He shrugged off his melancholy, reached for his glass. "Your suggestion has possibilities. What do you think?" This last to Esther.

Esther's right eyelash moved slowly downward in an exaggerated wink. "Simon's in his cups," she said. "He always gets this way when he's with people he likes. Ask him what he means. His proposition sounds vague to me."

"What exactly do you mean?" asked Fweeble.

Simon Crole blinked. "Did I say I liked you, Gus? No? It must have been Esther that put the thought in my mind. Well, I do. That's why I hate to spy on you. You showed courage out there in the driveway when you got out your flashlight and started to investigate something from which the ordinary man would have run away. That's one of the reasons I like you."

"I was scared," admitted Fweeble.

"I like the reverent manner with which you treat those bottles."

"I feel the reverence for what's inside of them."

"On that point we're agreed, Gus. Now listen, attentively. If you'll give me your word as a gentleman that you'll turn in a report of your nocturnal activities each noonday following, I'll revise them, make them seem perfectly harmless, and pass them on to your wife."

"Why should you do this?"

"To get rid of you," said Crole. "It isn't that I don't like to be with you. But I've got business that's more pressing. I didn't know I would have this business when I accepted your wife's case."

"There's a string attached to this somewhere, Mr. Crole."

"There is. For leaving you unmolested, and placing you on your word of honor to turn in some kind of a report each day, I place your case on the same basis as that of your wife. You pay a flat rate of a hundred and fifty a day for the services of my agency."

"It sounds involved."

"I thought I put it plainly."

"You did."

"Well," broke in Esther, "if you are going to talk business all evening, I'll have to hunt up someone to take me out on the dance floor. That music is too entrancing to merely listen to."

"Wait," said Crole. "I'll take . . ."

August Fweeble was already on his feet. The jaunty look had returned to his face. "May I . . ."

Esther took his arm, but not before the lively little man had bent down and whispered into Simon Crole's ear: "I'll accept your proposition. Gentlemen's agreement." He extended his hand.

The big detective got to his feet so that Esther could get past him. "Gentlemen's agreement," he repeated, taking the other's hand in his own.

Crole settled back in his seat after Esther and her escort had moved out onto the dance floor. He was thinking. Mr. and Mrs. August Fweeble were off his mind. One balanced the other. All he had to do was to sit tight and collect three hundred a day. He smiled his smile of perpetual surprise.

There was now Nicky Lombardo to consider. He knew that as soon as Lombardo found himself in the hospital he would close his mouth tight. He'd do no more talking. This meant that the police would have no reason for connecting him with the National City affair.

King would keep his mouth shut. And so would Larkin, unless the dicks from headquarters made it too hot for him. But who was the third man—the driver of the coupe? Was he the man Nicky had called "Mark"?

These questions and a great many others were still churning around in his mind long after he had seen Esther home and had returned to his own apartment.

He mixed a nightcap, rolled a cigarette, put on a flowery lounging robe and made himself comfortable. There were newspapers on the table that he hadn't, as yet, read.

He opened them now and went over every item of police news. The Larkin trial was moving to a swift conclusion. Public enemy number one had just been exterminated in a running gun battle. A lumber baron's boy had been kidnapped in Oregon. The famous hammer slayer, labelled by the press: *"The*

Tiger Woman", had just been released from the women's prison at Tehachapi for a long parole term. But there was no mention made of Larkin's confederate that Crole could discover.

What he did find, however, was the name and address of the cashier who had developed into the prosecution's star witness. He made a note of the address in a small book not unlike that used by Mark Schilling.

Then he swallowed his nightcap, yawned and pulled out the light.

His head had no more than touched the pillow when the phone rang. He grunted sorrowfully, got out of bed, and took down the receiver.

"Crole," snapped the voice of the district attorney. "What do you know about the shooting at the Green Gate roadhouse this evening?"

"Me? I don't know nothing, Mr. District Attorney. I got there too late. I saw the bodies. One man was dead. The other, critically wounded. I went in the roadhouse and told the manager. He called the police."

"See anything of any weapons? You didn't by any chance pick up a—say a .38 calibre gun, did you, and forget to turn it over?"

"Nope. I didn't see any gun."

"You saw the car, I believe, that the third man escaped in? What year and model . . ."

"I saw a car all right; had to jump into some bushes to keep from getting run over. It came down the drive without lights. I was too concerned in keeping myself from being run over to bother with year and model."

"You must have formed some idea, Crole."

"It was a coupe. As for color or make I couldn't even make a guess. It went by me too fast."

"You know, Crole," went on the district attorney, portentously, "it strikes me as odd that you should be in the driveway at the exact moment a killing is pulled off. This sort of thing has happened before. I'm getting a little tired of it."

"So am I," yawned the private detective. "But there don't seem to be anything I can do about it."

"If your foot has slipped this time, Crole, you won't have

to do anything about it. I'll handle that part myself."

"Don't be vulgar with your insinuations, Minifie. They won't get you anywheres with me. If you think you've got something on me and are prepared to prove it, then send a cop up to get me. Otherwise keep a civil tongue in your head."

The district attorney coughed. "I didn't meant to rile you, Crole. But I'm trying as a public prosecutor to get a little information out of you. No one else was remotely near the spot when the shooting took place except—oh yes, Captain Jorgens forgot to get the name of the man who was with you, the man with the flashlight."

"That's too bad," said Crole, secretly pleased at the police captain's error. "I didn't get it either," he lied, flagrantly. "It wasn't my business to handle the witnesses. If that's all, then good night."

"Good night," sighed the district attorney.

Crole hung up softly. "Doesn't that prosecutor ever sleep?" he complained to the darkened room.

4

NOTHING BUT JUSTICE

THE wall panel leading to the dentist's office had opened quietly. Michael Bemus stepped into the inner sanctum of the policital boss. "Hello, Mark," he said, dropping heavily into a big chair.

The fat man behind the desk eyed the police officer pleasantly with his pale eyes. He knew Bemus for what he was—a grasping, selfish man whose hand was always reaching out for more—and more. A man who would never be satisfied. A man you could trust only so far. A man without character or conscience.

"They got Nicky," said Bemus. "A lead slug in his chest.

'And a motorcycle cop was bumped off."

"One thing at a time, Mike. Who got Nicky?"

"That's what the D. A. would like to know."

"Where did this happen?"

"The Green Gate roadhouse. Outside on a parking lot. There was a third man in a coupe. He got away."

"How does the cop figure in this?"

"The way we dope it out is this: The cop, Danny Malloy, was following this coupe to give the driver a ticket for speeding. He caught up with it when the machine turned into the drive of the Green Gate. Nicky must have been nervous and got out his gun. Maybe he was thinking about the National City. Anyways, both were shot. The cop died immediately. Nicky's in the hospital in bad shape."

Mark Schilling turned all this over in his mind. "Who was with Nicky last night?"

"That's what the whole force is trying to find out."

"No one knows, eh? A hell of a note."

"Ain't it, though."

"You said the third man drove a coupe. Get a description of it?"

"There was only one man who got any kind of a look at it. In the dark he couldn't see it very well, and it was moving fast when it passed him with its lights out."

Mark Schilling grunted. He clasped his pudgy hands on the desk top. "Mike," he said. "I don't like this business. With Larkin about to be sentenced, and everything dropping from the papers, I figured things would quiet down."

"I figured the same way," agreed the police officer.

"Do the police connect Nicky with the bank stick-up?"

"I don't know. Haven't heard. Never can find out what the D. A. has in the back of his mind."

"District Attorney Minifie is out of your class," said Schilling. "I'll handle him myself when the time comes. Any guns found, clues, or anything like that?"

"Not a weapon of any kind. The whole business is kinda funny. I'll swear that Malloy had nothing on Nicky. The only way he could get anything would be through our office. And I've watched things damned close."

"It's funny all right," acknowledged the fat man. "Damned

funny. I don't like it. I don't like anything about it. Are you still with me, Bemus, or have you begun to welsh?"

Lieutenant Bemus laughed immoderately. "Know any more jokes like that, Mark? Say!" He leaned forward, jaw outthrust. "Don't you suppose I know what side my bread is buttered on? Don't I know that you've got more things on me than I like to think about? I'd be a fool, Mark, to cut myself loose from your organization."

"You're quite right, Bemus. If you ever cut loose from me, it would be the last thing you'd ever do. You belong to me as surely as does this desk. Play the game according to my rules, and you collect heavily, as you have in the past. Cross me —well, you know the answer."

The forehead of the police officer beaded with sweat. He wiped it away with the sleeve of his coat. "What's the next move?" he asked.

Schilling's pale eyes were thoughtful. "About this man who saw the coupe leave the driveway of the roadhouse. Maybe we'd better check back on him."

"I've done that already. Minifie talked with him over the phone last night. Jorgens also put him over the coals."

"Anyone I know?"

"Yes. The most notorious private dick in town—Simon Crole."

Schilling moistened his lips. "Simon Crole, eh?" He half closed his eyes. "There's a man, Bemus, I'd give anything to bring into the organization. I wonder how much he knows."

"Plenty without any doubt. But nobody can buy him, Mark, unless he wants to be bought. He works inside the law. Make no mistake about that angle. We've tried to nail him for working too close to certain statutes. A hell of a lot of good it did us."

Mark Schilling smiled affably. "Your police methods leave a lot to be desired, Bemus. In most ways they're crude. You haven't any finesse."

"Sure. I know. But that private dick is tricky."

"Figure he had anything to do with the shooting?"

"If he had," scowled the police officer, "he certainly wouldn't come clean with Captain Jorgens who questioned him only a few minutes after the cop was killed. Said he came there to eat and drink—which he does to perfection. He had a good-looking jane with him and an elderly man. The man is probably a client who is about to be nicked for plenty."

Schilling nodded. "I'll handle Crole myself for reasons of my own." Annoyance pursed his lips. "I don't like the idea of his being mixed in this business. I think it would be worth your while to drop into his office later and warn him to lay off. It strikes me that he's liable to prove a menace to the organization."

"My advice," spat Bemus, a trifle bitterly, "is this. Either buy him off at his own price, or bump him off."

"You think he's as dangerous as that?"

"I'm telling you, Mark If you and Simon Crole start a private war, one or the other will leave town—either on foot or in the back of a hearse. I know from my police experience."

"From what I know of Simon Crole . . ."

"I'm trying to tell you what *I* know. You've seen him around town. You know of him through other people. He puts on a good front. His reputation, while it isn't exactly sour, isn't sweet either. He's got more brains than any dick on the force. That's the truth."

"Has he got a big organization?"

"Big? Hell, no. Just a jane secretary and an operator with the mentality of a flatfoot. That's all he's got. But don't underestimate either of them." He lunged to his feet.

"Got to beat it," he said. "Lots of work to do. I'll call you later if anything new develops."

"You do that," said Schilling. "By the way, Mike, what hospital did they take Nicky to?"

"Good Samaritan. Why?"

"Nothing. Just wondered—that's all."

But Mark Schilling wasn't just wondering out of idle curiosity. Every thought in his fertile mind had a meaning behind it. As soon as the panel had closed behind the back of the police officer, he picked up the phone.

"Marie," he spoke to the girl with the steel-trap mouth at the switchboard "I want you to locate O'Brien. You'll probably be able to reach him at the Casino, or at the Little Chicago poolroom."

"I'll get him," promised Marie.

"Tell him," said Schilling, slowly, "to go at once to the

Good Samaritan hospital. Tell him Nicky's there. Wounded badly. Have him find out who the man was who drove the coupe last night. Nicky will know—if he's conscious enough to know anything. Get it?"

"Okay."

Schilling hung up. Waited a minute, then took down the receiver again. "Get me the office of Simon Crole, private detective. You needn't tell him who's calling. I'll talk with whoever answers."

Etta's bland voice came pleasantly over the wire a minute or two later. "Hello. Who is it please?"

"I want," said Schilling, "to talk to Mr. Crole."

"He's busy now. Who will I tell him is calling?"

"Tell him a man wants to talk to him about a coupe."

There was a distinct pause at the private detective's end of the line. No voices were to be heard. No sound or movement. Schilling, of course, could not look into the room where the receiver was off the hook. Had he been able to, he might have seen Simon Crole rubbing his bald head and muttering: "Man about a coupe, eh? And he won't give his name. Listen, precious," this to the secretary. "Is that wire chief still a friend of yours? He is? All right. Get busy on the pay phone downstairs. Trace this call."

He went back to the telephone again as Etta scurried out into the hall clutching a nickel in her fingers.

"Simon Crole speaking," he said.

Schilling hugged the instrument close to his chest. "Never mind whom I am," he began. "I called to see if you'd be interested in a certain coupe."

"I don't drive," said Crole, stalling for time. "I use cabs."

"You misunderstand me," purred Schilling. "I said a *certain* coupe. The one that nearly ran you down in the drive of the Green Gate roadhouse last night."

There was a long pause. Then Crole's voice. "You aren't by any chance the owner or driver of the coupe, are you?"

"No. But I know, or will soon know, who was driving the car last night. Does this mean anything to you?"

"In a way—yes."

"The information, in cash, is worth how much?"

"Precisely nothing. But wait. Have you talked with District

Attorney Minifie? You might try him. The coupe means nothing to me, aside from a slight professional interest."

"I see. Then you're not in the market for the tip, eh?"

"Right."

"Thanks," finished Schilling, hanging up. He set the instrument on the desk, lighted a cigar, and closed his eyes. So that was the way it was. Information in cash was worth precisely nothing. The coupe or its driver was likewise valueless aside from a slight professional interest.

Maybe the private dick wasn't interested after all. Perhaps Bemus was crediting him with something that didn't exist.

The door of his office opened. She with the steel-trap mouth stood just inside, closing it after her. "I talked with O'Brien. He's on his way. He'll call back as soon as he gets the information you want."

Mark Schilling nodded. "A-huh."

"Jensen," she continued, "the National City cashier, is in the waiting room. Want him sent in?"

"Jensen, eh? Anybody with him?"

"He's alone."

"Send him in."

Jensen entered, resplendent in a pin-stripe suit. His face was pale from long hours inside the bank. A small, needle-pointed mustache ran along his upper lip. He carried a stick, and seemed quite sure of himself and his ability to get along in the world.

"How are you, Schilling," he nodded. "I received your note and got away as soon as I could. What's on your mind?"

Mark Schilling grunted, twisted into a more comfortable position and fingered one of his three chins. "*You*," he said.

"Me?"

"Yeah. Been thinking quite a lot about you lately. Bank examiners show up yet?"

"They were here yesterday and part of today."

"Records clear?"

"Mine?"

"I wouldn't know about anyone else's but yours. They were in bad shape last time you were here. So were you."

"Oh! I had almost forgotten. That was fixed up the same day I was here."

"That's nice. Mighty nice." He tapped off the ash from his cigar. "You know, Jensen, I had an interesting talk with Larkin. Case you don't know Larkin, he was the one that pointed the Tommy gun over the edge of your window and ordered you to shell out."

"I was a witness at the trial. I know all about him."

"Not everything, Jensen. You know how much you handed him through the grille?"

"Roughly two hundred thousand dollars."

"Jensen," snapped Schilling, leaning forward with his fat elbows pillowed on the desk, "you're a liar!"

The cashiers eyes were bleak as two chunks of ice. He rubbed a moist tongue on lips grown suddenly dry. "You're mistaken, Schilling."

Schilling's lips twisted into a leer of contempt. "Jensen, I mean exactly what I said. I've talked with Larkin. I wanted to help him, to furnish him with a lawyer. He isn't a bad guy at heart. I thought he needed a hand and offered my help, but he said he preferred to take what was coming to him."

He paused and pointed a fat finger at the cashier. "There's a little item of a hundred and sixty-five thousand dollars that was never taken from your bank, Jensen—at least not by Biff Larkin. I know. Every nickel taken by Larkin was recovered intact, in the same bag you thrust across the window ledge. Ain't that nice?"

Jensen said nothing. His lips moved, but no sound came from them.

The brow of the fat man puckered in thought. "I suppose the best thing to do is to turn you over to the police."

If the venom in the cashier's bleak' eyes could have turned into water, it would have run in a stream down his cheeks. "I wouldn't ào anything like that, Schilling, if I were you. You've nothing to gain by it."

"Nothing but justice. It's like this. Larkin knew he was risking his life and liberty when he held up your bank. He played his cards from the top of the deck. He earned that thirty-five grand he got from you. Too bad he couldn't keep it. Worth that for the time he'll spend behind iron bars."

He paused again. "But you . . . you're nothing but a small time crook. You're making a fall guy out of Larkin. Well, I'm not going to allow you to get away with it, Jensen. It's against my principles."

There was an air of pious urbanity on Schilling's moon face. He wagged his great head back and forth on the column that was his neck and remarked judiciously: "I can't, Jensen. I can't allow you to do this monstrous thing to Larkin."

"And the alternative," asked Jensen, "if I refuse to play ball with you and split . . ."

"I mentioned no alternative," said the fat man, looking up suddenly. "What gave you that impression?"

"Nothing that you've said. But I know you, Schilling. I know your methods. You're no more honest than I am. Justice? Hell, it's just a word in your vocabularly. Let's get out in the open. How much do you expect to get out of this?"

"You've got me wrong, Jensen. I only want justice. By the way, how much have you got left?"

Jensen wet his lips. "I had a hundred and sixty-five to begin with. A little better than fifty thousand. went back into the vaults to cover my shortage. Ten thousand went for debts outside the bank, I've got about a hundred and five thousand clear. I'll split with you, Schilling, on condition . . ."

"I'm writing my own ticket, Jensen. Now listen. You're free of debt. You've got a good job. And you should, with your bank training, be quite well off financially with the five thousand. The hundred thousand I will take."

He rubbed his pudgy hands together. A rumbling chuckle caused the rolls of fat on his great body to flow like waves beneath his tailored clothes. "Do we understand each other, Jensen?"

The cashier swayed unsteadily to his feet, felt slightly sick, and sat down again. He could feel himself being squeezed between two jaws of something more punishing than metal. He thought of the enormous risk he had taken when the idea had first occurred to him, and the ease with which he had accomplished his theft. He thought—and the thought caused his heart to crowd up in his throat—that no one would discover his deception. But this pale-eyed, mountainous chunk of flesh knew. He knew beyond a shadow of doubt. How . . . how was he to get out of this man's power?

"If," he said in a barely audible whisper, "if I agree to your terms, Schilling, how will I know you won't cross me later?"

The fat man eyed his victim coldly. "Where is the balance of the bank funds?" he asked.

"In a safe place where no one will find it."

"In a safety deposit box?"

Jensen hesitated. "No."

"You go home," said the fat man, "and get it ready. I'll send a man to collect. As soon as he returns with it, I'll get in touch with you and we'll talk terms. I make no other promises."

It was then that the cashier realized that nothing he could say or do would be of any help. In the end Mark Schilling would get everything, and he—grey walls and iron bars formed a misty blur before his eyes.

He lit a cigarette to cover a momentary confusion. Cunning had reasserted itself now that he was driven to the wall. Maybe there was yet time to escape the net Schilling had drawn so tightly around him. He would go to his apartment at once. Recover the hidden currency. Then take a taxi to the nearest airport. Better a narrow freedom with plenty of money to spend, than to remain forever in the power of this fat monster.

He got to his feet a second time. He masked the cunning gleam in his eyes by lowering his lids. "I guess, Schilling," he acknowledged, "that your way is the only way out for me. I'll be glad to get rid of it. The stuff has been on my conscience. I haven't been able to sleep."

The fingers of the fat man tapped absently on the desk top. "In case I haven't made it clear, Jensen," he said, "I'll expect you to go straight home Speak to no one on your way. And stay in your room until my man arrives."

Jensen nodded. "I'll do as you say." He put on his hat, and walked out the door for all the world like a beaten man.

Schilling pressed a button. A rat-faced man entered from the contractor's office. His hands were white with long, tapering fingers. Had he appeared in a police line-up he would have been variously recognized by several names. But whatever the alias, his nickname clung to him. He was known as "Strangler". And he was Schilling's number one strong-arm man.

"Jensen just left," said the fat man. "Grab a cab and get to his apartment and wait for him to arrive. You know what to do then. He promised to give it up without a fight. He was lying. I could read it in his eyes before he thought to mask them. Remember, no noise—and no mistakes."

"Strangler" nodded. "Leave everything to me, Chief. There won't be no noise the way I handle him—and no mistakes."

When Jensen attempted to close the door of his apartment, something blocked it. His eyes jerked frantically over his shoulder. And he knew then why the door would not close. A man with a weazened, rat-face had crowded into the opening—a man he had never seen before. Something told him that Schilling had guessed everything that he had planned. Escape was cut off. He was beaten.

The shock was severe for the cashier was no hardened criminal. He realized in one blasting second that there was no avenue open to the freedom he had thought was his. The few minutes he had hoped for—only the time necessary to gather together a few things including the precious package of currency—these minutes were gone. They had never existed.

Numbness settled down on his mind. Paralysis destroyed his memory. The sudden shock had robbed him of all emotion. Whether he lived, or whether he died did not seem important. Apathetically he slouched into a chair.

He did not hear Strangler close the door. He did not see him pull on light cotton gloves so there would be no fingerprints left behind. Nor did he see him remove a coil of half-inch rope from beneath his coat. Even had he seen these preparations, it would have made little impression on him. He was beyond caring one way or the other.

"All right," said Strangler in a thin voice. "Hand over the money, and hand it over quick. I ain't got all night."

Jensen remained immovable, his jaws slack, his eyes wide open and staring.

"Hey!" Gloved fingers stung the cashier's face. "Wake up, guy. Don't try to pull any nut stuff on me. You hear?"

Jensen did not hear.

Strangler's eyes narrowed. He knotted his fist and hit the cashier under the ear. The blow knocked the man over backwards. He moaned from his sprawled position on the floor. "Leave me alone," he said.

"So," said the rat-faced man. "You ain't talking, eh? Well, I'm gonna make you talk, see? I'm gonna put a little pressure on your neck that will make that tongue of yours hang out a yard."

The rope curled snakily as he tossed it over a six-inch ornamental beam running lengthwise of the room. One end of the rope was already formed into a noose. Strangler inspected it, and went over to the cashier who hadn't moved from his sprawled position on the floor.

The body of the cashier was almost rigid. Strangler scowled as he lifted it to a table and adjusted the noose around the doomed man's neck. "Gonna talk now?" he asked.

Jensen made no sound.

"Hell," snapped the rat-faced man. "You look nearly scared to death. Then why don't you talk? Tell me where you got the stuff hid and I'll leave you alone. You hear me? Oh, you still want to hold out on me, huh? Maybe you think I don't know how to loosen the tongues of guys who won't talk. Try going without air for a minute."

He hauled on the rope. Jensen's body straightened till his toes barely touched the top of the table. Strangler threw a half hitch around the handle of a closet door.

Someone pounded on the door. The rat-faced man cursed and moved soundlessly toward it. He noticed for the first time that the window shade, only a few feet from the door, was not all the way down. He hugged the wall so as not to be seen in case whoever was outside looked in through the window.

The knocking continued. Strangler cursed himself for not thinking of that window shade. He looked towards his victim. A gasp escaped his lips. The body was slightly curled up with the feet no longer touching the top of the table.

After a time the person at the door moved away. Strangler went over and climbed to the top of the table. He was too late. Jensen was dead.

He climbed down again and looked at his victim. He couldn't understand how a man could strangle that quickly. But Jensen was dead, and he hadn't revealed the hiding place of the money. That was all right, too, the killer thought. He'd find it himself. But first he'd fix things to make it look like suicide.

The pale eyes of the fat man were unbelieving: "So Jensen kicked off while you were over near the door trying to keep out of sight in case anyone looked in the window?"

"Sure. That's the way it was. And so help me, the guy croaked before I could get back to him. I looked over every inch of the place but couldn't find a nickel anywhere."

"Strangler, you're lying. Come clean."

"Aw, why should I lie. I'm telling you exactly how it was."

"He may have strangled like you said, but you . . ."

"Say, you think . . ."

Mark Schilling nodded. "I think you're trying to pull a fast one on me, Strangler." His eyes became opaque. "I don't like men around that cross me up. I'll give you till tonight to turn over to me what you found in that apartment. Now get out!"

Mark Schilling watched his number one man go through the panel into the contractor's office. His mind was made up. He knew that there was only one answer to the problem. Men like Strangler were not to be trusted for long. Strangler's time was up—now.

A flicker of light from the ceiling announced a caller who was beyond the panel through which Strangler had just passed. Perhaps the man had decided to change his mind. Schilling smiled, and pressed one of the buttons beneath the desk blotter. The smile faded.

Gat O'Brien slunk through the panel. He came close to the desk as if afraid of being heard by someone outside.

"Well?" said the fat man.

O'Brien grinned. "I saw Nicky, Chief. He was in bad shape. The nurse wasn't going to let me in. But when I slipped her a couple ten spots I got in like nobody's business."

Schilling said: "Was he able to talk?"

"Sure. It was him what done the shooting all right. But get an earful of this. I told you that Judge Chadwick was a hard, tough baby. And I kinda hinted that I'd like to turn on the heat. Well, it won't be necessary. When I tell you the name of the guy what was with Nicky last night, you're gonna call me a liar. But I ain't lying, and Nicky ain't having no pipe dream. The guy's name is . . ."

Mark Schilling raised his finger to his lips. "Write it down on this piece of paper, Gat."

His pale eyes bulged slightly at sight of the two words his henchman had scrawled on the paper. Whistling softly, he applied a match to the paper and thrust it in the ashtray.

"It appears, Gat, that I've got a strangle hold on the Judge."

O'Brien reached for a cigar from the box on Schilling's desk. It was on his mind to take three or four on the strength of the report he had brought in.

"One's enough, Gat," reminded the fat man. "Them cigars cost money. And I don't like the idea of you being too promiscuous with anything on my desk."

5

THE HOWLING CORPSE

ETTA had rouged her cheeks, powdered her nose, and, with apparent carelessness had adjusted a red toque at a rakish angle above marcelled locks. "How do I look?" she asked.

Simon Crole regarded her pretty face without enthusiasm. "Charming," he nodded. "Utterly charming. But what's the idea, precious. You aren't running out on Simon, are you?"

"Dear man," said the girl, "must I go through this inquisition every night? I've been here since eight this morning. It's after six now. Don't I have any rights in this office?"

"If you do, you're the only one who does. Did Ridley get back from Yuma yet?"

"The plane doesn't arrive till eight."

"The plane? What's the matter with the rattler. Aren't trains good enough for that guy?"

"You wired him yourself to take the plane."

Crole consulted his watch. "I forgot. Well, it's later than I thought, and I still got a lot to do."

"You'd better go home yourself, old dear. You look pretty seedy."

"I need a drink," Crole told her. "Then youth and glamor will assert itself in this old hulk of mine. Run along."

"Bye," called the girl from the hall door.

"Bye," said Crole.

He took a sack of tobacco from his pocket and built a cigarette. He was thinking of Etta's friend, the wire chief, and the check-back on the person who had called his office about a certain coupe.

"So," he mumbled to himself. "Nicky's friend turns out to be none other than Mark Schilling who learns through the police that I was at the Green Gate when the shooting started. What, exactly, did he have on his mind when he called?"

He couldn't decide. Schilling was a big man, politically. It was rumored that he controlled several judges, and even had a certain amount of prestige in the D.A.'s office. Had Schilling been trying to draw him out in the interests of the police, or had he a strictly personal reason in wanting to know where Crole stood?

The paths of the two men had never crossed. Crole hadn't any desire to test the fat man's strength. He respected the political Boss's power. He had no intention of antagonizing it, or the man who controlled it.

"Damn," he frowned. "I wish that fellow King hadn't come to my office. I haven't a thing to gain out of the mess but a bunch of grief."

He took out his little book and memorized the address of Jensen. "Tonight," he told himself, "I'll go up and see this cashier, and have a talk with him. Then there's the Fweeble report to make out. And Matt coming back tonight with an expense account as big as a . . ."

The knob on the hall door rattled. Simon Crole got up, crossed the floor to his secretary's office and opened it. "Come in," he said to the police officer in the hall.

Lieutenant Michael Bemus shook his head. "Nope. Haven't the time, Crole. I came to deliver a warning."

"A warning?" The private detective knocked the ash from his cigarette to the floor. "Sounds natural coming from you,

Bemus," he grinned. "Is Captain Jorgens on his ear, or something?"

"Lay off," snapped Bemus. "Is that clear?"

Simon Crole shook his head. "No. It isn't clear, Lieutenant."

"I'll make it clear. Keep away from the National City case and everyone connected with it."

Simon Crole grinned stupidly. "What gives you the impression, Bemus, that I'm involved in the National City affair?"

"It's just a feeling I have, Crole, that you're trying to horn in and squeeze a fat fee out of somebody or other the way you always do."

"You cops down at headquarters are a sketch. Always suspicious. But you over-rate my abilities. I wish there *was* some way I could horn-in on this case. Fees appeal to me. Always did."

"I've warned you," threatened Bemus, his face reddening. "Stick to your divorce and scandal cases, and leave crime to the proper authorities. If you don't . . ."

"Then it'll be just too bad," finished the private detective.

"Exactly."

"Could I offer you a drink before you go?" asked Crole.

"You could," said the police officer, thinly, "but I'd turn it down."

"Too bad, Lieutenant. You're missing something rare."

Lieutenant Bemus turned away without another word and clumped down the hall towards the elevator. Crole closed the door. Waited till he heard the clang of the elevator door, then returned to his private office.

"There's a copper," he muttered, taking a bottle and glass from the bottom drawer of his desk, "who's got a bad conscience. He doesn't trust anybody—not even himself."

He rinsed the glass after he had finished his drink, and returned it with the bottle to the desk drawer. He then put on his hat, threw a final glance around the office, and went out into the hall.

There was a man, whom Crole recognized as belonging to the homicide squad, standing near the street entrance. The agency man was not pleased at the prospect of being followed. While he looked vainly for a cab the rakish machine of August Fweeble swung in towards the curb. From behind the wheel the old man called out: "Had dinner yet, Mr. Crole?"

Crole opened the door and climbed in. "Fweeble," he said, "it does my wicked heart good to see you." The car swerved from the curb and threaded its way through traffic. Crole looked back through a mirror fastened on the wind wings and saw the homicide man flagging a taxi.

"Fweeble," he said. "You ought to be glad you're not a private detective. The police are so jealous that they follow me around all the time. They don't give me a moment to myself."

Gus Fweeble kept his eyes on the boulevard. "If they are following you, and you were shadowing me, they'd be a lot of us going the same direction, eh, Mr. Crole?"

"Correct. Where are you taking me?"

"Most any place."

"There's a cab with a detective inside following me, Gus. It's about that shooting affair at the Green Gate. They figure I'm mixed up in it, and I can't seem to make them change their minds."

"I've been practising getting away from cars I thought were following me," said Fweeble. "I'm pretty good at it. Here's where we lose the cab." He twisted violently on the wheel. Shot the car into a driveway on the left side of the street. Was cursed by drivers moving in the opposite direction. Went into reverse, headed the car back where it came from, rode the next corner on two wheels, straightened the machine, and beat the changing lights at the next intersection by a matter of a split second.

When Crole looked behind, the taxi with the homicide man inside was no longer visible.

"Gus," he said. "That was a neat trick. I'll buy you a dinner and all you can drink for the favor."

"No," said Fweeble. "You're eating with me—at the Biltmore."

It was almost nine before Simon Crole managed to break away from the jaunty little man. Fweeble had wanted to know everything that was going on. He developed in the course of an elaborate meal an amazing technique of getting answers to a number of questions.

"A queer egg," mused the private detective. "Well, as long

as he's satisfied with our arrangement, I'm not going to suggest any changes."

He got into a taxi and gave the driver an address and settled back in the seat. Sometime later the machine jerked to a stop. Crole paid his fare and got out.

He found the number he looked for. Entered a courtyard; walked across some flagstones, and found a mailbox tagged: Charles Jensen.

He rapped on the door. No answer. He rapped again. Still no answer. There was a window to the left of the door. The shade was drawn, but not all the way down.

Crole went to the window. He took a flashlight from his pocket the size of a pencil. He held it against the window and peered inside. He could see overstuffed chairs and a table with a bottle and some glasses on it. He could also see, and what he saw caused a queer tingle at the base of his spine, a pair of oxford shoes. They were barely visible, and almost above the line of his vision.

But what impressed him most about those oxford shoes was their unnatural position in relation to other things in the room. They were apparently floating in space above a table.

The private detective left the window and approached the door. He rapped once more. Waited, then twisted the knob. The door opened. He slipped inside and closed it with his foot. He knew, then, as well as he knew anything, that he shouldn't have come. That he had erred. That he was too late.

Charles Jensen, crooked cashier, was dead.

From his position just inside the door, Crole studied the body dangling at the end of the rope, one end of which crossed a six-inch ceiling beam and was fastened to the knob of a closet door. He climbed to a chair for a closer look at the wood.

The beam had been finished with rotten stone to give it the appearance of age. He grunted at what he discovered, got off the chair and returned it to where it had been found.

He looked around. The room looked as if it had been thoroughly searched. A bedroom and a kitchenette had likewise been ransacked. He returned to the living room and its attendant confusion. First he examined the window by the door. It was locked, and the sill was covered with dust. He crossed the room to a second window.

There was a glass aquarium in front of it. Crole crowded behind the glass fish tank and examined the second window It was also dusty. He turned his attention to the carpet and to the scattered contents of desk and drawers, and drew a blank in each instance.

A trifle unwillingly he again examined the hanging body of the cashier. He could see limp hands. The fingers were long, tapered and immaculate. He looked closer. One of the nails had a deposit of something beneath it.

Crole turned away. Crossed the room towards the telephone. Changed his mind and returned. With the blade of his knife he removed the deposit beneath the dead man's finger nail and wrapped it in a cigarette paper.

Then with a clean handkerchief he wiped his fingerprints from all the objects in the room that he had handled, and noticed for the first time the wooden case that had once held beer bottles. His forehead puckered.

He turned towards the door beside which was a small table holding the telephone. The puckering across his forehead continued. He realized that if he called the police, he'd have a lot to explain. He also realized, with somewhat of a shock, that if the police later found out that he had been in this house of tragedy, and hadn't made a report at once, he'd have even more to explain.

He picked up the phone. "Police Headquarters," he told the operator. "Captain Jorgens," he said to the station operator.

There followed several minutes of waiting, then the voice of the police officer cracked over the receiver. "Police Headquarters, Captain Jorgens speaking."

"How are you, Captain?" said the private detective. "Simon Crole on the wire. Are you busy? No? Then get a couple of your boys, the morgue wagon, and come out to the apartment of Charles Jensen, 347 South Cedar Drive. Come and see for yourself. I'll be here waiting. Hell, nobody wants to run away. If I did, I wouldn't have called you."

He clicked the receiver in place and moodily rolled a cigarette. From a long distance down the drive he heard the moaning whine of the police siren. And then confusion in the court outside as the police captain and two of his men crowded through the door.

"The exhibit," said Crole, from the depths of a deep chair, "is suspended from the ceiling beam just the way I found it."

The black-lidded eyes of Jorgens took in the disordered room with swift appraisal. "Back up, boys. Don't walk around any more than is absolutely necessary. I don't want anything disturbed till the official photographer gets through."

He turned to the private detective, at ease in the deep chair. "Suicide, eh, Simon?"

Crole smiled lazily. "That's the way it looks."

"Hummm! I hope you've got a damn good reason for coming here and breaking into this man's apartment. If you haven't the D.A. will get to work on you. And I wouldn't give two cents for your rep after he gets through with you."

There was more confusion outside as the photographer and fingerprint man arrived. Behind them came Lieutenant Bemus, followed by a tremendous man with pale blue eyes.

"Evening, Captain," said the fat man, cordially.

Captain Jorgens nodded, and said gruffly: "Hello, Mark. How come you're . . ."

"I was talking with Lieutenant Bemus when the news came in. Had a speaking acquaintance with Jensen and was naturally curious. Mind?"

"Not at all. Mark, are you and Crole acquainted?"

Schilling's eyebrows lifted. "Oh, yes. We know each other professionally, but not through any business dealings."

Crole said, without getting up from the deep chair. "How are you, Schilling? Fancy meeting you here under these unfortunate circumstances."

Schilling's three chins quivered. He laughed softly. "They are somewhat unfortunate, Crole. Extremely. Poor fellow. Suicide is a terrible thing."

"Murder, too," grunted the private detective.

"Eh? Did you say . . ."

"Here's the medical examiner," said Jorgens. "About time."

A slim man with pop eyes, an idiotic sense of humor and a black bag had crowded into the room. "Ah," he said, his pop eyes fixed on the dangling figure at the end of the rope. "The daring young man on the flying trapeze. He's dead, Jorgens. Been so for at least two hours."

He climbed to the table top and examined the bloated face of the cashier. "Strangulation," he stated. "Victim died suddenly. Lips are drawn in as if he tried to speak before the rope choked him. Ummm! I see. He stood on that empty beer case, fastened the noose, then kicked the box off the table. Suicide, Captain, without doubt."

"You sure?"

"Well, figure it out for yourself. I can't make a thorough examination until I cut him down. He may have wounds on his body, but I don't think so. He died from strangulation."

Jorgens nodded. "Cut him down, if you've finished."

"Wait," called out the photographer, "till I get another picture." He adjusted his camera, stuck a flash-bulb into a near-by socket and turned on the juice. A blinding flare followed. "Oke," he said.

"Give me a knife, somebody," called out the examiner from the table top. "I'm not using my scalpels to cut this hemp."

A knife was passed up. "Get ready to grab him," ordered Jorgens to his men.

The cops got beneath the dangling body. "Ready?" called out the examiner. "Here's the corpse." The knife blade cut through the rope strands close to the victim's neck. They parted with a jerk.

Immediately a singular and gruesome thing happened. As the pressure of the rope around the throat was abruptly released, the mouth of the victim popped open. A sustained, bestial howl filled the room.

"Fi . . . eee . . . ooowww!"

The silence that followed was broken by a muttered oath from one of the men holding Jensen's stiff body. "Is he dead, Doc?"

The examiner jumped from the table. Every man in the room watched him, and waited for his second verdict.

"Of course he's dead. I know you heard the victim let out a sort of a howl. Well, it sometimes happens that way with a person who's been strangled. Air, breathed into the lungs a fraction of a second before the great air tubes are pinched tight by the action of the rope, is under pressure within the lungs. The moment this pressure was released the air comes rushing out of the tubes to the mouth. The sound you heard was entirely mechanical."

He said no more, but bent swiftly to his task of examining the body for other signs of injury. After a time he straightened, returned his instruments to the black bag, turned to Jorgens, said: "All physical indications point towards suicide."

Jorgens nodded. "Would the physical indications for murder be any different from those of suicide?"

"Not enough to detect. There's the box he stood on. His financial affairs may not have been entirely in order. That's up to you to find out. The certificate will be made out, unless you find something to the contrary, to suicide." He smiled, hummed a gay tune and vanished out the door into the court.

"Very interesting," chuckled Mark Schilling, "and highly instructive. That's the first time I ever heard a corpse howl. And I hope it will be the last."

"Suicide, eh?" snapped Jorgens, scowling at the length of the rope still hanging over the beam. "I don't like the looks of things. Something's not just right."

"Captain," said Mark Schilling, with just the right shade of reproval in his voice. "I'm afraid your constant association with crime inclines you to the silly belief that every death is caused by a murderer."

"Maybe you're right, Schilling. But my work makes me suspicious of everything and everybody."

"Stick to your guns, Captain," yawned Crole from the depths of the easy chair. "Jensen didn't commit suicide. He was murdered!"

6

THE MURDER CLUE

IN the shocked silence that followed there was no audible sound but that of men breathing.

Captain Jorgens turned slowly, his back to the table. His

lips moved jerkily as he bit off each word. "It might be just as well, Simon, if you kept out of this."

The ancient scar near Simon Crole's lips twisted his face into the look of perpetual surprise. "Sorry, Captain, if I spoke out of turn."

"You're always speaking out of turn," growled Bemus. "And butting in when you've got no business to. If I was Captain Jorgens, I'd smack you down and put you through a course of sprouts."

"Is it the usual thing, Captain Jorgens," asked Mark Schilling, indicating the private detective with his thumb, "for this man, Crole, to be present during investigations of this sort?"

"No," said Jorgens, biting his lip. "It isn't. We can handle this case without any outside interference."

"I'd suggest, then, that you order him from the room under the custody of one of your men."

"That's a swell idea, Schilling," grinned Crole.

"Unfortunately," said the police captain, "this private dick was the man who reported the hanging. I can't let him go yet. I've got a lot to say to him. And he's got considerable to explain to me."

He crossed the room and towered belligerently in front of the chair where the private detective sat. "So you think it's murder, eh? You're a smart fellow, Simon. Too smart for your own good. Maybe you'll tell us what makes you think this isn't a suicide."

"Maybe I would," said Crole, "if I was in the pay of the county. As it is, I'm a private citizen with certain rights protected by law. If you want to risk throwing me in the jug, go ahead. The investigation is in your hands. Likewise the responsibility of the police department. Hell, you got two eyes, the same as I have."

"I can force you to talk."

"No one said you couldn't. You could ask me all kinds of questions and I could say I don't know, or I forgot, or I don't remember."

"And you'd be lying!"

"Maybe so. I've a notorious memory." He got to his feet, and his face was within a few inches of the police captain's. "I don't see any reason for hanging around here any longer, Mr.

Schilling seems to think the investigation would run smoother if I was elsewhere. Well, I'm leaving, if it's all right with you, Captain."

The police captain chewed on the cigar between his teeth. "It's all right with me. But I'd advise you not to go too far from your downtown office. You're not finished with this case. Keep that in mind." ·

Crole said from the doorway: "I'm not likely to forget."

As the door closed behind him, Mark Schilling said: "Simon Crole seems very sure of himself, Captain. Do you think he's right about Jensen not being a suicide?"

The lips of the police captain twisted into a sour grin. "Simon Crole," he snapped, "is a sensation-monger. He's all bluff."

Mark Schilling shrugged his massive shoulders. "That's what I thought. All bluff."

"But don't overlook this fact," scowled Bemus. "He's also tricky. I wouldn't trust that guy in a poker game even if an honest man held and played his cards for him."

The man they were talking about was at this moment boarding a street car for the ride back to the darkened city. Never, during the rest of his life, he knew, would his ears be free from that howling cry of protest coming from the mouth of the corpse.

He noticed, as he fitted the key into the lock of his office door, that there was a light inside. Evidently his operator had returned.

Matt Ridley, Crole's operator, looked up from the report on which he was working. He was a tall, lank man with the shoulders of a coal heaver and the face of a third-rate fighter. He wore his hat on the back of his head. And his eyes were generally screwed up questioningly as if something in his mind was not quite clear—which was generally the case. He was altogether fearless, and loyal to the last heart-beat to Simon Crole.

"Hi, Boss," he waved.

"Matt," sighed Crole, grunting into a chair across the desk. "I'm glad to see your battered face again. It isn't much of a face, but at least it's honest."

"Don't send me down to Yuma again," said Ridley. "It's too hot. I'd like to sweat the hair off my head."

"Did you close the case?"

"Closed, sealed, signed and delivered."

"That's good. Well, the agency is involved in another case. It isn't anything I asked for. I was sort of drug into it, so to speak. I'll tell you how it all happened."

Briefly he outlined everything that had transpired during the past several days not forgetting to include the involved financial arrangement with the Fweeble family.

"Quite a sport, that old guy," approved Ridley. "He can take me to dinner at the Biltmore anytime he feels like it. After all the chili beans and tamales I've been guzzling the past week, I'm ready for a good old steak with plenty of young onions."

"Always thinking of your belly," sighed Crole, deftly rolling a cigarette. "Now listen, and see if you can remember everything I tell you without my having to repeat."

He took the cigarette from between his lips and peered at the slow-forming ash. "The biggest guy, politically, in this town is Mark Schilling. I won't go so far as to say that he controls the prosecutor's office and the police department because I don't know that he does. But he does wield a certain amount of influence. A damn sight more than I do.

"There's no direct way of obtaining any evidence on Schilling. He's too clever. Now. What I want you to do is to take up a station near the entrance to the Commerce building where the political boss has his office. Watch every man who goes into the building. You know most of the crooks in this town. If you see any of them enter the building, tail them. Find out what floor they go to—and if they visit Schilling in his office."

"It ought to be a cinch."

Simon Crole nodded. "Yes, it ought to be a cinch. And don't make yourself any more conspicuous than necessary. Maybe I'm all wet about Schilling. I don't know. And you'd better do something about that face of yours, Matt. Some of these mobsters might recognize you, and tip off Schilling. I don't want that to happen. It might spoil my plans."

Leaving Matt in the outer office, Crole went into his own. From a wall cabinet where he kept a morgue of interesting news items and photographs, he took out a folder from under the heading "S". He searched the folder until he found a rather thin envelope bearing the name of Mark Schilling.

"Poor pickings," he muttered, "but there ought to be something of interest in the meagre collection."

He took the envelope to his desk and began to go through it, muttering to himself as he scanned the items. "Ummm! Ward healer, councilman, supervisor. Then out of politics. Indicted with others in sewer graft. Released. No evidence. Sewer records removed from file clerk's office."

He rubbed his head and continued. "Heavy contributor to all charities sponsored by members of law-enforcement bodies and courthouse attachés. A good mixer, a spender. Friendly with big contractors. Owner of gambling salon known as the Casino."

Crole stopped rubbing his head. "The Casino! Hell, of course. That used to belong to Pokerface Smith." He returned the thin envelope to its proper place and took out folder C. Under this heading he found a list of clubs. Night clubs, gentlemen's clubs and dancing clubs.

In the typed list of gentlemen's clubs he found the Casino. He read aloud: "Swanky, evening clothes only, roulette, baccarat, dice and cards. No limit. Ladies admitted with escort. Admittance by card only. Clientele very select."

A knock on the hall door interrupted his labors. "See who it is, Matt," he called.

"Says his name is August Fweeble," called back the operator.

"Send him in and keep the door locked. 'Lo, Gus," he grinned at the jaunty little man. "How's tricks?"

"I'm fine, Mr. Crole, just fine. Got bored, so thought I'd look you up and see if you'd run into any more trouble from the man who was following you."

"I've had trouble," said Crole, placidly. "Plenty. But from an altogether different source. That's over with, temporarily. Listen, Gus. You look like a pretty good sport. You ever gamble?"

"Yes," admitted Fweeble. "I'm not very good though. I always lose." His eyes seemed to brighten at the prospect. "What have you got on your mind? I'm tiring of night clubs and floor shows."

"A select gentlemen's club. Excellent facilities. Fine bar. Handsome women. And no-limit games. How's it sound?"

Fweeble's eyes were uncommonly steady as they bored into Crole's. "Sounds all right. But I don't know as I care to risk too much money. After all I'm under a heavy expense as it is, what with paying you for services and paying the same amount for my wife."

Crole smiled ruefully. "I'm in a bad fix, Gus. Call off your wife. Make her see the error of her ways. Otherwise there's nothing for me to do but keep taking your money."

Fweeble smiled understandingly. "I'm not blaming you, Mr. Crole. Business is business. To get back to this other thing. You mentioned gambling. Do you want to see me lose money, or have you got some sort of—shall we say—chicanery up your sleeve?"

For no reason that he could account for, Simon Crole felt a genuine liking for the man who faced him across the desk. It wasn't pity, but actual respect.

"Gus," he said, "I'm only a private detective in a city that's lousy with politics, graft and crime. Politics and graft are not my line. But crime is. I'm mixed up in it now. So are the police. So is a certain potential enemy of mine."

"I see," nodded Fweeble, "but I don't yet understand what all this has to do with the club?"

"I'll get to that," promised Crole. "This potential enemy is, I believe the actual owner of the Casino. It's located in one of the older sections of the city, and is thoroughly respectable."

"I'm not certain yet what you expect *me* to do."

"You have connections, Gus. You could get a card of admittance. We could both get in on it."

"Do you really want to gamble?"

"Not so much as I want to get inside and look around. I want to study faces. I want to see how welcome I am in this particular gambling place."

Fweeble nodded. "And the name of your potential enemy is . . ."

Mild surprise was in Simon Crole's eyes. The jaunty little man was always asking such direct questions. "I can't tell you, Gus. It wouldn't be fair either to him or to me. I may be wrong you understand."

"Like the police, eh? I saw in the papers a mention of a funny little man with a flashlight. But they didn't have my name."

"The police captain thought of the oversight when it was

too late. He asked me, and I told him I didn't know. Didn't want your wife to know how close you came to being a murder witness."

"That was thoughtful of you, Mr. Crole. Well, I'll see what I can do about that card of admittance. I've got a few friends who know how things like this are done. What's the best night to go down there?"

"Saturday, Gus. And remember, it's a swanky place. No one admitted without evening clothes."

"Sounds almost too high-brow for me. But I'm sport enough . . ."

A commotion at the hall door caused Crole to glance up sharply. He heard Matt Ridley's voice, and that of Captain Jorgens. He grinned wryly on Fweeble. "Sorry, old top, it's the law in the person of the police captain himself."

Jorgens strode heavily into the room. "Evening, Simon. I guess you thought you were finished with me . . . oh! Well, I'll be damned, if it ain't the funny little man who had the flashlight the other night at the Green Gate roadhouse. Well, well, it looks like the party is complete.

"Good evening, Captain Jorgens," bowed Fweeble.

"I didn't get the name," said Jorgens.

"Fweeble . . . August Fweeble. Address, Langster Apartments, Ramona Boulevard. I'm glad to see you again. Are you making any progress on that traffic officer case? I haven't seen any reports of arrests in the papers."

"The identity of the cop killer," observed Jorgens, drily, "is known, and his arrest is expected hourly."

August Fweeble nodded. "I read that in this morning's paper."

"Carry on," said Simon Crole. "Honestly, Captain, you haven't been getting the breaks."

"Simon," growled the police captain, "haven't I always been square with you?"

"In your quaint way—yes."

"Jensen's dead," stated Jorgens, patiently. "Jensen was the cashier of the National City bank. Do you think, Simon, that there is any connection between his suicide and . . .?"

"Tsk, tsk!" clucked the private detective. "I'm trying to impress on your mind, Captain, that Jensen didn't commit suicide. Jensen was hung,—not by himself, but by someone who wanted his death to appear as a suicide."

"I heard you say something like this before, but I didn't ask for details. You can give them to me now."

"Did you examine the beam across which the rope was stretched?"

` "No. I didn't examine the beam. I examined the rope."

"Wrong answer. You should have looked that beam over. It holds the murder clue. If you had done so, you would have discovered that the friction caused by the rope being dragged across it had rubbed away its edge covered with rotten stone. You would also have found small strands of hemp imbedded in wood slivers."

Jorgens grunted and said nothing.

"If," argued the private detective, "Jensen had tied the rope around his neck while standing on a box placed on the table, and then had kicked the box out from under his feet, there wouldn't have been any friction marks on the edge of the beam. The reason is simple. There wouldn't have been any dragging rope to make those marks. Is my point clear?"

"Quite," said Captain Jorgens. "I'll have the photographer take some close-ups of that beam. But you haven't made it clear, Simon, why you went to Jensen's apartment in the first place. Was he a client of yours?"

Crole shook his head. "No. Jensen was nothing to me but a crooked cashier who profited on a bank hold-up to the extent of a hundred and sixty-five thousand dollars."

Captain Jorgens smiled glassily. "You think of everything, don't you, Simon?" His voice hardened. "Well, that's the angle I've been working on—who got the difference between the amount we recovered when we nabbed Larkin, and the amount reported lost by the bank."

"Jensen got it."

"Then where is the money now? And why was he murdered?"

"He was murdered for the money. That's perfectly obvious. But who killed him, and who has the money now, I wouldn't know, Captain. You'll have to admit that there was small reason to suspect Jensen of defrauding his bank. You weren't sure yourself or you'd have locked him up and hauled him over the coals."

Jorgens pawed at his bristle mustache. "I thought of it," he admitted. "I thought of it several times."

"So did I," said Crole, "but I was about an hour or two too late reaching his apartment. So that's that."

"You haven't," asked Jorgens, casually, "by any chance learned the identity of the coupe driver?"

"A guy called my office yesterday," said Crole. "Wouldn't tell me who he was. Wanted to know if I'd be interested in paying him for a tip . . ."

Jorgens' eyes were snapping with impatience. "And you . . . what did you tell him?"

A placid smile wreathed the private detective's face. "It occurred to me, Captain, that this man was from your office, or that of the district attorney. So I told him that the information was worth precisely nothing to me. I also suggested that he call Minifie's office, since the coupe meant nothing to me aside from a slight professional interest."

A dark flush spread over the police captain's face. "Simon, I'll swear by everything I own that you weren't being baited from either the D.A.'s office or my own."

"How was I to know? Besides, I didn't care much about butting into police affairs . . ."

"Go to the Devil," flared Jorgens. "You'd butt that bald head of yours into anything that promised a fee. Well, I wish you luck. But don't blame me if there's a kickback in this business. Minifie's getting hard to handle, and the press aren't any too friendly. So use your own judgment, and good bye!"

He left the office slamming the door behind him.

"This is all highly exciting," observed August Fweeble. "I think I'd better go home before the District Attorney comes."

Simon Crole got out his tobacco sack and papers. "Maybe it's just as well, Gus. I don't like these unpleasant scenes any more than you do, but they're part of the game."

August Fweeble put on his hat. "I'll see what I can do about that card of admittance. Then I'll call you on the phone, or drop in."

After the jaunty little man had left Simon Crole placed the rolled cigarette on an ash tray, wiped the moisture from his

forehead, and slyly opened the drawer containing his private
stock of Bourbon. Deftly he pulled the cork. It came free with
a slight plop!
 Ridley heard the welcome sound. Dropped all work on his
report and strolled into the inner office. "Bourbon," he approved, his eyes on the bottle. "Shall I get an extra . . . ?"
 "Yes," said Simon Crole. "Get a glass, and shut up!"

7

GUILTY

THE jury, after three hours of deliberation, had reached a
verdict. Solemnly it filed into the courtroom. The ruddy face
of the foreman—a ranch owner, was grave with responsibility.
There had been little doubt of the outcome after the first ballot.
He moistened his lips and faced the bench.
 Biff Larkin had faced his trial with a calmness not given
to most men. He had known what the outcome would be when
it slowly dawned on him that Mark Schilling was not going
to help him.
 He remembered, somewhat bitterly, others who had been
on Mark Schilling's payroll, and had suddenly been dropped
via the state prison route.
 He had kept his mouth shut about Nicky. He wasn't the
type that broke down easily. "Find out yourselves," he had
told the inquisitors as they put him through a course of mental
bludgeoning calculated to weaken him and loosen his tongue.
 No, the police had failed. Larkin had waved away the
promise of a lighter sentence if he would tell everything he
knew. He didn't believe the cops. He knew what he had risked
when he walked into the National City with a chopper under
his arm. He had no regrets—only a deep-seated bitterness
against the man who might have helped him, but hadn't.

Vaguely, as though from a great distance, he heard the voice of the jury foreman. "We find . . . the defendant . . . guilty . . ."

He was aware of a stir in the seats around him as morbid spectators turned their heads to see how he would take it. His face was in repose. He kept it that way.

His eyes were on a black-robed figure slowly rising to pronounce sentence. The voice was clear, scholarly. There was no personal animosity in its tones; no smug platitudes. Larkin listened attentively for a while, then his mind wandered.

He'd learn a trade while he was in prison—a trade like King's. Then, maybe, after he had served his time, he and King would go into business together. It wasn't impossible. It was even comforting.

Judge Benson Chadwick's closing words impinged on his ears like blows of a hammer. ". . . judgment of this court . . . sentence . . . you . . . ten years of hard labor . . ."

Larkin was rather glad it was over with. He smiled on the stern-faced judge to let him know he bore him no ill-will. Then the bailiff had him by the arm and was leading him away.

Alone in his chambers after court had adjourned, Judge Benson Chadwick scanned several briefs that would soon require his undivided attention.

His face was lean, long and clean-shaven. The hair around his temples was white. The rest was black. A stern man in all court dealings, dignified and proud.

Here was a man who had served long and honorably on the bench. Here was a man who couldn't be bribed. A man with ideals. A man of unswerving loyalty in the performance of his duties; a man whose inherent honesty was above question.

Here was a man who had weathered the storms of politics, graft and scandal. While district attorneys had fallen by the wayside from the blasts of grand jury investigations; while other judges had been dishonored, and with cause, Judge Benson Chadwick had never once been jarred from the pedestal on which the voters had placed him.

A faint knock on the door of his chambers caused him to turn slightly. "Come in," he called.

Mark Schilling entered. His fat face was wreathed in a bland smile. "How are you, Judge," he said. "Too bad about

Larkin, eh? I wonder how he feels now that he's headed for the state prison."

"Oh, hello, Schilling. Of course, Larkin, I'd forgotten the man. I suppose he feels like all the rest of them. I will say this much in his favor, he impressed me as being very much of a man. As a rule these gunmen are surly and contemptible. If he behaves in prison as well as he did in court, the parole board will give him a decent break."

"Busy?" asked Schilling, easing his hulk into a black leather chair.

"Never too busy if a man's business is important enough."

"Mine is important." His pale eyes studied the imposing face of the jurist. "But more important to *you* than to me. You won't thank me for coming to you. That's all right, too. But I thought it was time, Chadwick, that we came to an understanding.

Judge Chadwick smiled bleakly. "There can never be any understanding between me and the crowd you represent, Schilling. I thought I made that clear in the past."

"You did. That's why I never bothered you. But that time is past. As a matter of fact we're going to be good friends. You're going to help me, and I'm going to help you."

"And if I refuse?"

Mark Schilling's pudgy fingers toyed with his lower lip. "You won't refuse, Chadwick. Otherwise, I wouldn't have come to your chambers. I have in my pocket a photostatic copy of an original statement written by a man named Nicky Lombardo."

"He's the man," said Chadwick, thinking back, "who was wounded by officer Malloy?"

"The same," agreed Schilling. "He died at the Good Samaritan hospital this morning."

"Well?" The eyes of the judge were still bleak.

"But before he died," resumed the fat man, placidly, "he signed a written statement in the presence of two witnesses. And that statement is at present locked away in a place of safe-keeping known only to myself."

"There's more to come, I presume?"

"Yes, Chadwick, the interesting and somewhat unfortunate part is yet to come. But perhaps, you don't want me to continue. The button on your desk would bring a court attendant on the run, and you could have me thrown out on the sidewalk."

"I could do that, of course. In fact nothing would give me greater pleasure, Schilling. My feelings towards you I have never troubled to conceal. There is something fetid and bestial about you that assails my nostrils like a foul stench."

Schilling's facial expression never changed by so much as a muscle twitch. "Your feelings towards me, Judge Chadwick, are the least of my concern. Whatever they are, and whatever they continue to be will be your own personal affair. But they can't alter the fact that I've got you in a tough spot. You'll knuckle down to my wishes, or . . ."

"Are you threatening me, Schilling?"

"Not yet. Not till you know the facts."

"I'm waiting. And when you've finished, I'll have you thrown out, as you suggested." His voice quickened, took on a steel-like edge. "Go ahead. I'll listen to what you have to say. But make no mistake, Schilling. I'll never take orders from you or the group behind you."

"I started to tell you about that statement signed by Nicky Lombardo. Now listen carefully. These are sweet words, Chadwick, and damning to your name and prestige. It wasn't Nicky who shot Officer Malloy. It was someone else—it was the man who owned the coupe Nicky was in."

Judge Chadwick controlled his temper with a visible effort. "I still don't see how all this affects my relations with you."

Mark Schilling chuckled. His gross body quivered like a mass of jelly. "The man," he went on, unhurriedly, "who drove the coupe the night officer Malloy was bumped off was a friend of Nicky Lombardo. He's the man who killed Malloy. And that man was—Gordon Chadwick . . . your son!"

The knuckles of Judge Chadwick were white from the gripping tension he exerted on the edge of his desk. "Schilling, you're a liar. Now get out! Get out of my chambers before I throw you out bodily."

"Wait, Judge Chadwick! Wait. You don't suppose I'd be stupid enough to make such a statement without damn good proof, do you? If you won't examine this proof, there are others who will. District Attorney Minifie would give his eye teeth to lay hands on this statement of Nicky's. And so would the cops. They're sore. You know how it is when one of the boys gets bumped off."

Judge Chadwick paled. His lips formed a thin, straight line. And there was a faint twitching in his jaw muscles.

The fat man went on. "There's also the newshawks. This statement of Nicky's was made to order for those babies. They'd pounce upon it like a flock of harpies. You know how fickle public opinion is. Well, it would turn on you like a striking snake."

"Yes," said Chadwick, calmer now that the first shock had passed. "But Schilling, you know perfectly well my son . . ."

"Your son is no better than the rest of us. He liked his wine, women and song. He made a mistake though in picking up with a man like Nicky. Now listen, Chadwick. If I tip off the police right now they'll pick up young Chadwick and his car. And I'll lay you odds of a hundred to one they'll find Lombardo's prints inside that car."

"May I see this statement?" asked the judge, quietly.

"Sure. I brought it with me for just that purpose—so you could see just how things stood between us before I made any move against you."   .

He handed Chadwick a photostatic reproduction of Nicky Lombardo's damning statement signed in the hospital, and witnessed by a nurse and an interne. "Read it over," he said. "It's a genuine document, duly witnessed by two reputable people."

Judge Chadwick's hand shook as he took the document from the fat man. He read it slowly, word by word. And every phrase was like a shaft piercing his heart. Finally he finished and laid the paper on his desk. "May I keep, this copy, Schilling?"

"Why not? I can have hundreds of the same thing made without much trouble."

"May I ask how this came into your possession?"

"I suppose you can. And you'd have a perfect right in asking me. But for reasons of my own, I can't tell you." His lips puffed out. The lids of his pale eyes drooped. He watched his victim narrowly.

"I'll take it home with me tonight," said the judge, heavily. "You'll give me a little time, I hope, to think it over—say a week. I'd like to question my son. If he fails to satisfy me, I'll arrange a conference with you, and we'll decide then what's best to be done."

The fat man, suspecting trickery, hesitated. "Yes," he said, finally. "But your son will probably lie to you. Why shouldn't he? He's in a tough spot. Now listen, Chadwick. Keep away from the D. A.'s office. You might not find yourself as welcome as you think."

Judge Chadwick nodded slowly. "You're perfectly right, Schilling. This isn't a matter for the prosecutor's office or that of the police."

"Just so long as you keep that in mind," observed the fat man, heaving his great bulk erect, "there's no reason why we can't get together and work with reasonable harmony."

"I can't tell you, Schilling," sighed the judge, "how much this has hurt me." He closed his eyes and leaned back in the chair—a despairing figure of a broken man.

"See you later, Chadwick," called Schilling as he went out.

"Yes, yes, of course. We'll see a great deal of each other."

The pale eyes of the fat man narrowed for a moment. It was as if he sensed something wrong with the picture. But the feeling of uneasiness vanished almost at once. Judge Chadwick was still leaning back in the chair, his eyes closed, his lips twisted in a smile of bitter defeat.

For several moments after the door to his chambers had closed Judge Chadwick's eyes remained shut. Then they popped wide open. He got to his feet. There was nothing despairing in his attitude now. The bleakness had returned to his eyes.

He crossed the room. Opened the door. Looked out, then closed it and snapped on the latch. He went to his desk and thumbed through the telephone directory. His voice was the voice of a jurist who knew what he wanted and how to get it.

"Make the appointment at eleven," he told the person who had answered the phone. "And don't fail to have him in his office. It's highly important to me. Good day."

He hung up. Removed his robe of office. Stared thoughtfully at the photostat copy of Nicky Lombardo's statement and thrust it into a leather bag, along with the briefs of several cases that were slated for his court. He put on his hat and left the building.

He arrived home slightly earlier than usual. A manservant admitted him and took his hat and coat.

"Whiskey and soda, Jenkins. Bring them to my study. And I do not wish to be disturbed."

"Very good, sir. Dinner at the regular hour?"

Judge Chadwick nodded and went upstairs to a private study adjoining his bedroom. He placed the leather bag on a small desk, glanced momentarily around him, then went into his wife's room.

Everything was just as it was three years ago after she had smiled at pain and closed her eyes for the last time. It was the way she would have wanted it. Each article in its proper place. Flowers in vases. Windows open so that the curtains stirred softly.

Her picture in brown sepia beside the dresser mirror seemed alive as he looked at it. There was a gentle warmness in the eyes—a sort of a mute understanding. The lips of a wide mouth were closed. But they smiled. Judge Benson Chadwick squared his shoulders and bowed. It was part of a nightly ritual.

He went into his son's room. There was no way of telling if Gordon had slept in his bed the preceding night. No way of knowing unless he questioned the maid. But Judge Chadwick never questioned the servants on the goings and comings of the boy.

Back to his study he went. Whiskey and soda were on a tray beside his desk. He filled a tumbler and drank slowly. Finished, he opened the leather bag and took out the statement of Nicky Lombardo.

He read it again, sighed, and placed it in his pocket. He got up and opened a small safe. From a folder he removed the adoption papers he and his wife had received when they had brought a two-year old child into their home and named him, and with pride, Gordon Chadwick.

"Mother, young, strong and healthy," he read, as he had read these words many times in the past. "Father unknown, but believed to have come from a good family. Hereditary charactertistics not yet determined. The right environment should develop all the excellent qualities from the mother's side."

The adoption papers crackled as they were returned to the

envelope. "There was no way of knowing how the boy would turn out," murmured the judge. "We have treated him as if he were our own. But I'm afraid the boy has failed . . . No! I won't believe it. Not yet."

He got to his feet and paced nervously back and forth. His eyes were bleak again with the banked fires of anger as his lips formed three explosive words: "Gross . . . fat . . . toad!"

8

A DISTINGUISHED CLIENT

JUDGE BENSON CHADWICK walked heavily into the agency office as though the worry on his mind had suddenly turned into a physical weight. He took off his hat upon arriving at Etta's desk and said: "I have an appointment with . . ."

"Mr. Crole is waiting for you, Judge Chadwick. Please step through this door." She pointed with a manicured hand, and pressed a warning buzzer with her knee beneath the desk.

Simon Crole, his lips slightly askew, was leaning forward over his desk. His grey eyes were scanning a typed report a messenger had brought to his office but a few minutes previous. It had come from an Austrian chemist whom Crole had once helped in a small way. Inside the folded report was a cigarette paper containing the material found beneath the fingernail of the deceased Charles Jensen.

The report was brief. It merely said, without comments: 'Silicon, quartz particles, black sand, dried fronds, commercial black lacquer and minute quantities of green sealing wax.' It was signed: 'Mueller.'

"Huh!" he grunted. "All that stuff under a man's fingernail. But what does it lead to? Silicon, quartz, dried fronds. From a fern or something." He shook his head sadly. "Interesting from the standpoint of a geologist perhaps, but no good for a private dick."

He placed the report away in the drawer and promptly forgot all about it until sometime later when the eerie howl of a corpse was again profaning his ears.

He looked up questioningly as Judge Chadwick entered. "Have a chair, Judge." His voice was soft and pleasant. He wondered, idly, what was back of this unusual call.

"Thanks." Chadwick placed his hat carefully on the desk, then sat down. "Simon," he began, "I'm in trouble."

"You? In trouble? I can't believe it."

"Nevertheless, I am. And the trouble is serious."

"I'm sorry to hear you speak like this, Judge." His face broke into a reassuring smile. "I'm also in trouble. The police in this town are beginning to ride me hard. We don't get along. Well, let's get on with *your* troubles, judge. Mine is always with me."

"What do you know about Mark Schilling?"

"Me? Considerable. And yet, come to analyze my knowledge, I really don't know much of anything about him. But the police would know. They have a source of information . . ."

"Never mind the police," broke in Chadwick. "They're efficient, capable, and for the most part, honest in the performance of their duties. To go to them would mean failure at the very start. My career on the bench would be a closed chapter. I can't go to them, Simon. It's impossible. In the jargon of the underworld, I'm about to be placed on the spot. I'm helpless."

"I've failed at times myself, Judge Chadwick," said Crole.

"I've thought of that, too. But I've known you for a long time, Simon. I know that you've solved a number of the city's most perplexing crimes, but that the credit has always gone to the police. You no doubt have your reasons for not wanting to show your hand in these solved mysteries. That doesn't concern me. What does concern me is this: I need your aid."

"And the case has nothing to do with the police?" queried Crole.

"The police might enter into it if you didn't. In that event Mark Schilling would have succeeded in smashing me."

"You'll trust me then, when you won't the police?"

Judge Chadwick's keen eyes attempted a smile. "Your

methods, and those of the police are not the same. While you have always remained within the law, there have been times . . ." He paused. And his keen eyes achieved their smile.

Simon Crole also smiled. "Yes," he admitted. "There have been times, as you say. But my service runs high, Judge."

"I expect to pay—and pay an exceptionally high price."

"Fair enough. What's your problem?"

Judge Benson Chadwick reached into his pocket and took out the photostatic copy of Nicky Lombardo's statement. "Here," he said. "Before we get down to essentials, I want you to read this document and draw your own conclusion as to how it came into my possession, and why it was delivered to me."

Simon Crole rolled a cigarette, lighted it, and spread the paper on his desk. His forehead creased with concentration wrinkles as he read:

Of my own free will, and because of my fear of the hereafter, I, Nicky Lombardo, am making the following statement:

On Tuesday noon, September 13th, me and Biff Larkin held-up the National City bank. Later, when I leave Larkin, after we fixes a meeting place to split the dough we'd lifted, I met Gordon Chadwick. His old man is Judge Chadwick. But he seemed like any regular guy at that.

We got in his coupe and drove to the Green Gate road-house where I had a date with a moll. Chadwick drives so fast that a cop takes after us. He's right behind us when the car turns into the parking lot outside the roadhouse.

Chadwick said to me: "Watch me croak this cop." I says: "Don't. What do you want to do that for?" "I don't like cops," he says.

The cop sticks his head in the car window just as the machine slows to a stop. "Where's your driver's license?" he asks.

"Here," says Chadwick. He hauls out a snub-nose rod. So does the cop. The cop's bullet misses Chadwick and hits me. Chadwick fires. Twice. I see the cop kinda sag

*and drop. Then I falls against the door which I had un-
latched. That's all I remember till I'm in the hospital.*

Signed:

Nicky Lombardo

*Witnesses:
May Latimer, Nurse
Dr. John Worth, Interne*

Simon Crole pursed his lips. "Quite a document. Schilling bring it in to you in person?"

"Yes. He allowed me a week in which to make my decision. He plans to corrupt my court whenever it pleases him. If I don't do as he orders, he threatens to turn this statement over to the police."

"Ummm! Tell me something about your son."

The face of Benson Chadwick twisted in a grimace of pain as if Crole had probed an ancient wound. "Before God, Simon, I don't think Gordon is capable of anything so vile and despicable. But what is my belief against a man's voluntary statement attested to by two witnesses?"

"Never mind the statement. I'll handle that when the time comes. Tell me about your son."

Judge Chadwick partly closed his eyes as if better to visualize his son. "Gordon," he said, "was always difficult to handle. But my wife, before she died three years ago, loved him as if he were her own. We gave him everything—perhaps more than we would if he had been our own flesh and blood. I tried not to be too severe with him. I helped him over many of the rough spots. But there were parts of this boy I could never reach. We never quite understood one another."

"I see. What I'm expected to do, as I understand it, is to recover Lombardo's original statement from which the photostat copies were made to save your son . . ."

"To save my son," repeated Judge Chadwick, grimly, "if he's not guilty. I trust we understand each other."

"I think we do," said Crole. "What I'm trying to get straight is my own position in this case. I can appreciate your reason for not wanting the police messing up this business. But I'm bound to cross them before I get very far."

He paused for emphasis. "Now listen, carefully, Judge. And

don't for a single moment forget what I say. No matter what happens whether because of the police, or through the machinations of Mark Schilling, my first and only interests will be centered around the recovery of this statement of Nicky Lombardo. Is that point clear?"

"Quite."

"It means a state of war between me and Schilling with no holds barred. Pay no attention to the reports you may hear concerning me and my methods. I'll keep within the law as far as it is humanly possible. But I won't hesitate to go outside of it if Schilling forces me to do so. He has an organization. I have one operator and a few friends I can bank on in a pinch."

"Whatever happens, Simon, I'm relying on you to see this thing through to a finish."

"To a finish, Judge. Now, will you arrange it with your household so that I can make an examination of your son's room when he isn't home?"

Judge Chadwick nodded. "Anticipating your request, I have spoken to my manservant. Gordon didn't come home last night. So far as I know, he is still away. You can go to my house and make your examination any time you wish."

Crole grunted. "Ummm! I'll take a run out there this afternoon and get it over with."

Judge Chadwick got to his feet. "I guess that's all."

Crole nodded. "I guess it is. For the present at least." He went with the judge as far as the door leading into the hall, shook hands with him, told him not to worry, then closed the door.

Had he followed Chadwick after the judge got out of the elevator on the main floor and left the building, he would have seen a certain police lieutenant follow his client to the first corner, then stroll slowly down the street towards the nearest telephone pay station. Lieutenant Bemus, at the moment, was not working for the police department. He had other irons in the fire. The number he called was answered at once by the telephone operator with the steel-trap mouth.

Unaware of all this, Simon Crole returned to his desk. His grey eyes were thoughtful. Nicky was dead. But in death he had placed a powerful weapon in the hands of an unscrupulous man. Or had he? Suppose, for instance, that statement had originated in the fat man's office? Crole scratched the lobe of his right ear. He shook his head. No. Schilling would never make a mistake like that.

He finished with the lobe of his right ear and made tentative overtures towards the left one. But suppose Schilling had made a mistake? It was possible. Everybody did the wrong thing some time in their lives. He decided to keep this angle in mind.

It was close to noon when Ridley came in, flushed and disgusted. "Boss," he said, "There's something phoney down at the Commerce building."

"Yeah? See anybody you knew?"

"I saw a guy named O'Brien. You remember him—a short, thick-set guy known as 'Gat'. Well he comes to the building and eases in the street door. And I'm right behind him. He gets off at the fifth floor where Schilling has his office. But he don't go in. Instead, he breezes into a contractor's office which is close by."

Ridley paused, then continued. "I takes a look around like as if I got off on the wrong floor then gets back into the elevator, goes up one floor and comes back again by the stairs. I hides in a washroom where the porter keeps his mops and closes the door all but a crack.

"Pretty soon O'Brien comes out and gets in the elevator. While I'm still there among the mops and pails, I hear the elevator door slam. And there's that mean dick, Bemus."

Crole's eyes blinked rapidly. "Bemus, eh?"

"Yeah. I thought maybe the dick was tailing O'Brien. But I guess he must have had a bad tooth or something. He went into a dentist's office. I hung around awhile, then slipped out of the washroom and come down the stairs."

"There's something wrong with the set-up," observed Crole. He rubbed his bald head to stimulate thought processes. "Matt, while you were gone, Judge Benson Chadwick was in." Briefly, he recounted what had taken place. "Now," he finished. "There's nothing definite to work on but the boy, Gordon, And that'll be my job."

"You want me to go back to the Commerce building again?"

"No." Crole shook his head slowly. "The thing is too risky.

Someone who knows you would be sure to spot you and report it to Schilling. That wouldn't do. I don't want to tip off my hand yet. Tell you what I want you to do. You go and see the superintendent of the building opposite the Commerce. Tell him you're looking for a single room with windows facing the street. And if you can find such a room on the fifth or sixth floor, grab it. Take a lease if necessary under somebody else's name. But make certain that the windows face those of Schilling's office.

"O'kay. And how will I close the deal?"

"Cash, Matt. Find out first how much you'll need. Etta will take care of the rest. She can also arrange for some second-hand furniture. And if I can get hold of Esther, I'll establish her there as your secretary so that everything will appear regular."

"That sounds all right to me," said Ridley. "I'll beat it down there and see what I can do."

Sometime after his operator had left, Simon Crole got up from his desk and went into the front office. "Etta," he said, "Matt's gone out to rent an office. He'll come back after a time for cash. Give him a cash check on the Security-First National. And get hold of second-hand furniture, and arrange for a telephone."

"You kidding me?" asked the girl.

Crole wagged his bald head. "Nope, I'm dead serious."

"What's the idea?"

"Mark Schilling is too far away, precious. I want a place where we can watch the comings and goings in and around his office. In other words, I plan to get a line on his organization through the only way I can figure—direct observation."

He picked up the phone and called a number. "Miss Manning please. Hello, Esther? Simon Crole. You're working for me again. Same rate on a twenty-four hour basis. I know you've got a job, but listen. I need you. Maybe you've got a vacation coming. Tell them you're sick. Tell them anything. Listen, woman, I've got to have you. It's about that affair at the Green Gate. Yeah, it's had its repercussions and bounded back to my office. And listen, keep Saturday night open. I'll tell you later, G'bye."

He grinned on his secretary. "Esther is working for us

again." He reached for his hat. "I'm on my way to Judge Chadwick's home. But you needn't tell anybody where I've gone."

He put on his hat, grinned slyly at his secretary and went out the door.

The home of the judge was in an exclusive suburb where buildings were far apart, out of sight from the street, and generally surrounded with fences of concrete or wire.

An elderly manservant answered his ring. Simon Crole explained who he was, and the purpose of his call.

"If you'll step inside, sir," he said. "Judge Chadwick phoned instructions to admit you whenever you came, and to help you in any way that I could. Care to visit the young man's room now, sir?"

Crole nodded. "He isn't home, then?"

"No sir. Haven't seen him for several days. Kindly step this way, sir, and up the stairs."

After they had arrived at Gordon Chadwick's room and the manservant had vanished into the lower regions of the house, Crole made a swift examination of the whole upper floor including the judge's room, his wife's, and the position of the back stairs.

He then went to young Chadwick's room. He examined clothes closets of which there were two. One filled with beach garments, sweaters, bathing suits and worn tennis shoes. Evidently, young Chadwick spent a good portion of his time at the beaches.

Still, that signified nothing. Crole's fingers went deftly through pockets. It wasn't till they reached a faded green bathrobe that they came in contact with a folded oblong of paper. He opened it. It was a redemption slip issued by a loan broker. Crole pursed his lips, refolded it and tucked it in his pocket.

From the closet he turned to a small desk. Rapidly and expertly he went through the drawers. Note paper, envelopes, loose-leaf notebooks from an eastern college. He snapped them shut and pulled on the center drawer. It was locked.

He frowned. Took a ring of keys from his hip pocket and was on the point of inserting one in the lock when he heard a slight sound in back of him. He whirled, and found himself confronted by a sandy-haired young man holding an automatic in his tanned fingers.

Crole said without any sign of embarrassment: "Where did you come from?"

"Who, me?" The sandy-haired man had a brittle voice. His teeth were white against the tan on his face. "I just walked in the back way to get a change of clothes. I live here. This is my home."

"You're Gordon Chadwick?"

The young man nodded. "And you?"

"My name's Crole . . . Simon Crole. I'm a friend—a particular friend of your father's, Judge Chadwick."

"Maybe you are," said young Chadwick. "Then again, maybe you're not." The gun still pointed unwaveringly at Crole's chest.

"I'm glad you turned up," said Crole, helping himself to a cigarette from an open box on the desk. "Now lay aside that gun before it pops me in the lungs."

"Cool customer, aren't you?" His voice took on an edge. "What's your business here in my room?"

"A fair question," said Crole. "I was looking for you."

"Sounds reasonable, but did you really think you'd find me in that desk drawer you were trying to unlock when I came in?"

"Smart boy. Do I look like a thief? Put up that gun. Or something similar to what happened at the Green Gate the other night might happen again."

Young Chadwick paled. He moistened his lips and backed away. "You . . . I don't get your meaning," he said.

"I didn't expect you would. Listen, Chadwick. What made you draw a gun and kill officer Malloy?"

Chadwick backed still farther away. The gun in his fingers trembled. He sat down slowly in a chair and allowed the gun arm to drop to his knees. "I see," he said, a little helplessly. "You're from police headquarters."

Simon Crole shook his head. "Wrong. I've got nothing to do with the police. I told you I was a friend of your father. I told you the truth, Chadwick. And I like to be your friend."

Gordon Chadwick laughed mirthlessly. "Why?"

"I'm that way," said Crole. "Your father is about to be smashed politically because of something you've done."

"It's a lie," flared the boy, lurching erect.

"Sit down, Chadwick. You and I are going to have a talk."

Chadwick relaxed and tossed the gun to the desk top. "I don't want to talk. I want to be let alone."

"Sure. I know how you feel. But I've got to talk. It's part of my business. And you're going to sit and listen and answer yes or no to my questions."

"Why should I answer your questions? I don't know you."

"You don't know me," said Crole. "But you will. Listen. You knew Nicky Lombardo was dead?"

Chadwick nodded. "Yes."

"But did you know that before he died he made a statement in writing blaming you for the murder of officer Malloy?"

Stark, unreasoning fear glittered in the boy's eyes. "Nicky ... Nicky said ... I ... killed ... the ... officer?"

"That's what the statement says, Chadwick. And he signed it at the hospital in the presence of two witnesses. Oh, it's all regular and quite damnable. You admit you were driving the coupe ... ?"

"I ... I ... yes, I guess I was. Yes. It was my car. Nicky was with me. But I swear ..."

His voice stopped short. Through the abruptly opened door came Judge Chadwick. And behind him, like a portentous shadow, waddled the fat man, Mark Schilling, his pale eyes flecked with red.

9

A SEVEN DOLLAR TICKET

THERE was a moment of strained silence.

"Well, well," rumbled the fat man, stroking his jowls with a dimpled hand. "Simon Crole. Can't I go any place in this town without running into you?"

"I wonder," mused the private detective. His mouth twitched. Surprise was on his big face. This wasn't so good. There was trouble back of this sudden visit—trouble for both the judge and himself. Mark Schilling was cunning. Wary. He was playing his cards fast. Crole shook his head sadly. "We do seem to be getting into each other's way. That's the way it looks."

Schilling's eyelids drew close together. "I don't like you, Crole," he said, bluntly. "You might as well know it now for all time. Get out of this house, and stay out."

Crole said without moving. "Just like that, eh? Aren't you taking a little too much for granted in ordering me around?"

"I'm sorry this had to happen, Mr. Crole," broke in Judge Chadwick. "But . . . well, the fact is, I've changed my mind about . . . ah, certain things. Mr. Schilling objected in a way to my going to an absolute stranger for advice. And he's right. I see, now, that I made an unfortunate mistake."

"A swell time to find it out," raged the private detective. "Hell, it puts me in bad all around. I've got no grievance against Schilling. But it makes enemies out of us when I want to be friends with the guy. Politics! Damn it, I'll never take another case like this. I'm cured—forever!"

"Then out!" ordered Schilling.

"With pleasure," bowed the agency man. "Luck to all of you —bad luck, and plenty of it."

"I'm sorry you feel this way about it," frowned the judge. "But believe me, Mr. Crole, I'm acting for my best interests. Be so kind as to send me your bill for services and I'll have it taken care of immediately."

Crole's grin was derisive. "My bill? Sure I'll send it. I'd be a sap if I didn't. But I'm washing my hands of the whole business. I'm out—finished. If the kid swings for the murder of officer Malloy, then it's just too bad all around." He stormed out the door into the hall, and slammed it violently behind him.

But once in the hallway, all anger vanished from his round face. Coolly he glanced the length of the hallway. It was empty. He hesitated no longer than a triple heart beat; clumped noisily down the stairs; opened and slammed the front door. Then, with that feline grace that marked his every movement, he ascended the stairs, glided past the closed door to young Chadwick's room, and let himself into the room sacred to the memory of Judge Chadwick's dead wife.

He stood for a moment in the center of the room, wary, alert, hands on hips, listening.

The door from young Chadwick's room opened and closed. There was a sound of footsteps along the carpeted hall leading towards the judge's room. The murmur of voices was indistinct.

Simon Crole crossed the room to a connecting door. The house was old, paneled with wood half way to a high ceiling, and there was a transom above the door. It was open.

The voices became distinct, as the three men entered the judge's room. Schilling was talking.

". . . unfortunate indeed, Chadwick, but the error is yours."

"We'll go over that later," said Judge Chadwick. "My first concern is to question Gordon. Have chairs. Sit down, Gordon. No sense in pacing the room. After all, whatever difficulties you're in can be straightened out."

Crole edged closer to the connecting door.

"Now listen, Gordon." This was the judge speaking. "Were you out at the Green Gate roadhouse the night the traffic officer was shot?"

"Yes, I was. I had my coupe. A friend of mine, Nicky Lombardo was with me."

"Nicky Lombardo died in the hospital, Gordon. But before he died he made a statement accusing you of murdering the traffic officer."

Gordon Chadwick was silent.

"Well?"

"I don't believe I killed the man."

"Then there's doubt in your mind?"

"I had too many cocktails that afternoon. Everything was in kind of a mist. I remember driving Nicky to the roadhouse. But as I drove into the place I got suddenly sleepy. Then my mind went blank. The next thing I remember I was driving down the highway without lights. I switched them on. I was trembling all over. I knew something awful had happened. But I didn't know what."

"Did you shove Nicky out of the car?" asked Schilling.

"I don't know."

"What did you do with the gun? It wasn't found by the police either on Nicky or on the ground. You . . . you must have found it in your coupe later. Am I right?"

"I didn't see any gun or find any."

"Don't lie about the weapon," warned Schilling. "There *was* a gun. Two bullets from that gun were dug out of the dead cop's body. Ballistic experts can identify that weapon once they lay their hands on it. It's calibre is already known—a .38."

"I've got an automatic," said young Chadwick. "It's on my desk. But it's smaller—a .32. I said I didn't know any weapon being in my car. I don't."

Schilling accepted the last statement with a snort of derision. "But you admit, Chadwick, that you and Nicky Lombardo were together when you drove into the parking lot of the road-house. You'll have to admit, also, that a cop was killed from two bullets fired from the interior of your own car, and that you immediately drove away. Your actions on that night were not those of an innocent man."

"I'll admit everything but the shooting of the officer. I can't believe I'd kill a man unless my own life was in danger."

"That, of course," said the fat man, judiciously, "is the weakness of your story. Your belief—and remember, you weren't sober at the time—wouldn't carry much weight in court. The prosecution would rip it to shreds. You're guilty, Chadwick, and you know it. I think the best thing for me to do is to turn this evidence over to the district attorney's office."

"Schilling," said Judge Chadwick. "I wouldn't do that if I were you. You've nothing to gain. You'll bring ruin and disgrace to both me and my son."

"Ruin," purred the fat man, "is something that comes to all men. Suppose, for instance, that the district attorney knew what all three of us know. Suppose he knew, also, that I suppressed evidence in a murder crime. Not nice to contemplate, is it? And yet that is exactly what I was ready to do, to protect you and your son. I offered you a chance to protect yourself. You accepted. Then you crossed me by going to this private detective."

"I tell you again, Schilling, that I went to Simon Crole for only one reason—to get his advice. I thought he might be of help to both of us."

"Simon Crole," said the fat man, acidly, "is notorious for being of help only to Simon Crole."

The private detective blinked at this estimate of his greed. It occurred to him that Mark Schilling was, in a manner of speaking, somewhat notorious himself along these lines.

The voice of Judge Chadwick again reached his ears. "The point you raise, Schilling, is perfectly clear in the matter of suppressed evidence. But I'm pleading with you as only a father can plead for his son. I ask you to reconsider. I can do no more. Tell me, what do you propose to do?"

"That, Judge, is up to you. It depends on how willing you are to play my game. Chadwick, you can go back to your room while your father and I talk this over. But remember, keep your mouth shut. Don't talk to anybody. Maybe it would be just as well if you lammed out of town for a couple of weeks until this storm blows over."

"Dad," said young Chadwick. "What'll I do?"

"I think Mr. Schilling is right. You'd better go. I'll see you in a few minutes regarding financial arrangements."

The door to the hall opened and closed. Crole heard the shuffling feet of the boy move down the hall. The voices coming through the transom resumed.

"You've got to do something about this, Schilling. That boy means everything to me. And I don't want him to suffer."

"Quite so. But you'll have to give me time to think it over, Chadwick. The risk, you know, of suppressing valuable evidence."

"I understand all that."

"There's that private dick to consider. Something ought to be done about that man. I don't trust him."

"I'll pay him off, and that will be the end of him."

The fat man grunted. "Good. Well, I'll run along. Get the kid out of town. We'll decide then what's to be done. Meantime, Chadwick, the Shapiro case opens in your court sometime this week."

"Tomorrow."

"Shapiro is innocent."

"But Schilling. Consider the evidence."

"I still insist that Shapiro is innocent. Listen. The prosecutor can easily be curbed by a good judge. I shall expect you to give all the breaks possible to Shapiro's lawyer. Acquittal is certain."

Judge Chadwick's voice was curiously flat. "I see. I'll do

whatever I can, Schilling. Yes, I'm quite sure that Shapiro can be acquitted."

"The defense fund is heavy," said the fat man. "I can promise you five thousand for the right kind of a verdict."

"No, thanks. I wouldn't take Shapiro's money . . ."

Schilling laughed thinly. "Don't be squeamish, Chadwick. We're all in this thing together. And Chadwick, it might be wise if you'd come to my office whenever we have anything to discuss. Fifth floor of the Commerce building. I can assure you that no one will listen to anything we have to say to each other."

Crole heard the door to the hall opening. Their voices became indistinct on the front stairs. He gripped the door knob, turned it, and let himself into the hall. No one was in sight. He went down the back stairs. Eased out a service door, passed through a gate and reached a side street.

At a corner drug store he called a cab company and asked for a certain driver. The driver and cab reached the corner a quarter of an hour later.

Crole climbed in. "George," he said to the driver. "There's a man in a coupe who'll soon be backing out of that driveway near the corner. Tail the coupe and don't lose it. There's a five-spot in it for you besides whatever's on the meter."

"Okay, Mr. Crole."

Five minutes passed. Ten. Then the coupe, black with chromium trim, backed into the side street, and turned around. When it swung down the avenue, Crole's taxi was not far behind.

The coupe stopped some minutes later at the Pacific Electric ticket and bus station. Crole leaned forward and spoke to the cab driver. "Follow that kid to the ticket window and find out where he's going."

The driver returned in a short time. "He bought a one-way ticket for Crown Beach."

Crole nodded. "Good work, George."

Meanwhile young Chadwick had returned to his car, removed two bags and was taking them to the station checking room. Then he got into his machine again and drove to a storage garage where he checked in the coupe. He didn't return to the station, as Crole thought he would. Instead he stood outside the storage garage as if undecided as to just what to do.

Simon Crole had no further interest in the boy just then. He knew where he could find him if necessary. So he spoke again to the driver. "Take me to the four hundred block on Main."

Here, he dismissed George Scavillo's cab. Found the loan broker's establishment, and went in. He took the folded slip of paper from his pocket and placed it on the counter. The proprietor looked at the number on the ticket, then at the private detective. He went into a room in the back of his store. He returned after a minute with something wrapped in paper.

"You aren't the man who brought this in," he said.

"No," said Crole, "but that man was a friend of mine. He asked me to redeem it for him."

"It'll cost you a month's interest plus a carrying charge—seven dollars altogether."

Crole laid the money on the counter and took the package. As he thrust it in his coat pocket he knew he had a gun—an automatic by the feel.

From the loan broker's place he walked to the entrance of his own building, but a short distance away.

Etta was mildly excited as he closed the door. "Matt rented an office," she said. "And I've ordered the second-hand furniture. It'll be delivered in the morning. You've got an intelligent staff, in case you don't already know it."

"Intelligent is not the word, precious. Superb more correctly describes you and Matt."

He sat down in a chair near her desk. Took out a handkerchief and mopped his bald head. "Events move on," he mused. "Sometimes they're good, sometimes not so good. Evil overcomes the just. Graft and corruption reach new high points. But virtue has its own reward."

Etta glanced at him sharply. "Are you strictly sober?"

"Strictly, my dear. Take a letter. The Honorable Judge Benson Chadwick. Dear Judge Chadwick: Confirming your instructions received at your home this afternoon, comma, I am closing your case as of this date, comma, and attaching herewith a statement of charges as you directed. Period! Cordially, no, don't use that word. I'm not supposed to be the least bit cordial. That's a fact. End it with yours truly. The hell with the cordial stuff. Excuse that violent four-letter word, precious."

Etta said without looking up from her shorthand notes. "Not knowing the facts, it would seem that difficulties have arisen."

"Yes and no. But as I remarked, virtue has its own reward. Make out a bill for five-hundred bucks for service."

"Too bad," sighed the secretary, shaking her pretty head. "That case should have netted the office at least five-thousand."

"Eh? Too bad? Nonsense. Make out the bill as I directed, and cease your observations. Leave everything to Simon."

"Then the case isn't closed?"

"Did I say it was?"

"Excuse me for living. I seem to remember taking down in shorthand that you were closing the Judge's case."

"I said *that?*"

"Quite distinctly."

"Then it must have been what I meant to say. Send the letter as dictated. And don't forget the bill for five-hundred bucks. This office is going to be under heavy expenses the next few days."

He got up and went into his own office. He fumbled in the desk drawer for tobacco, papers and Bourbon. The telephone rang just as he got everything set out. He scowled and took down the receiver.

"Hello," he said. "Yeah, this is Simon Crole. Who? Oh, King. How are you, King? What's troubling you? Yeah . . . you saw in the papers that the cashier of the National City committed suicide. Well, well, I saw the same thing. A-huh . . . the hell you say . . . you think he was murdered? Maybe he was. That's a smart thought."

He eyed the bottle of Bourbon moodily. "How you fixed financially, King? Could you use a couple of hundred bucks? You could? No, I'm not offering you a bribe. I want you on *my* side."

He caressed the Bourbon bottle with his fingers. "They's gonna be some questions raised in police circles about you being Larkin's friend. You know how those things get around. The cops haven't forgotten that slight discrepancy in what the cashier actually pushed over the counter, and what he reported as being taken. That slight discrepancy of a hundred and sixty-five grand is causing more than one guy an acute headache."

He pursed his lips and waited for King to get in a word.

"Sure," he continued. "I get your angle. But you see, King, how it is. Larkin comes to where you work directly after the bank job. Maybe somebody saw him. You don't know. Then you come to my office. See? And then what happens? I'm at the cashier's home reporting his death only a short time afterwards. A vicious circle any way you look at it. One thing ties up with the other."

He paused to let that sink in. "That's the way it is," he went on. "So, if any broad-shouldered guys with big feet come mooching into your place to question you, just forget everything you know about your friend who took his rap without squealing. And forget also, that you came to my office. See? Right now my secretary is putting two hundred bucks in a plain envelope. And that envelope will be delivered by Uncle Sam to your house."

The protest was weaker at the other end of the wire.

Crole said: "It's a case of business with me, King. You gave me a good tip. I'll cash in on it. And it's only fair that I treat you white. Now keep your mouth shut and everything will be jake. Okay."

He hung up. Went to the front office. Told his secretary what to do with two-hundred dollars and returned to his desk. He rolled a cigarette and lit it. Then poured himself a drink. He drank slowly as one who enjoys flavor more than effect.

He leaned forward, elbows on desk, chin cupped in the palms of his hands, his eyes focused dreamily on the empty glass. It was about time, he thought, to start a slight agitation in the public prints.

After a time he got to his feet. "Precious," he told his pretty secretary. "I'll be right back."

"Where you going?"

"Pay station where I can use a telephone."

"What's the matter with our own line?"

"Our own? It's tagged with my name. This call I'm making I don't want traced here."

"Sounds like skull-duggery to me."

"Believe me, precious, it is."

10

THE BOY RETURNS

SIMON CROLE left his office and took the elevator to the street level. He went to a pay booth a short distance down the street and dropped in a nickel. "Schuyler 2560," he spoke into the mouthpiece. "Hello, *Ledger* office? I want to talk to the City Editor. Hello, Farrel?"

There was a pause. Crole went on. "Never mind who's talking. I got some points your sheet ought to play up on three city crimes. Oh, you're not interested unless I give my name, huh? That's okay with me. I can pass them on to the *Examiner* if you think they're too hot."

Again a pause. The voice at the far end of the wire said: "Go ahead."

Crole went ahead. "Question number one: Who got the remainder of the two-hundred thousand taken from the National City bank? Only thirty-five thousand was recovered by the police.

Question number two: Who was Larkin's pal on the bank job, and why have the police failed to trace him? Officer Malloy knew. But Malloy was rubbed out just as he was about to make a pinch."

The voice of the editor said: "Keep going ahead."

"Question number three: Why was the cashier of this same bank murdered . . ."

"Wait a second, Mister. Did you say murdered? The Medical Examiner's report indicated suicide."

"Keep in mind the missing hundred and sixty-five thousand," said Crole. "Good bye." He hung up and left the booth.

He went out to the street and saw a man in a gray suit and purple tie lounging at the curb close to his office building. He thought he recognized him as one of the district attorney's men. But he wasn't positive.

"Haven't I seen you before?" asked Crole, pleasantly.

"Who, me? Naw."

"S'funny," said Crole, still smiling pleasantly. "You look like a certain gent from the public prosecutor's office."

"Yeah? What's funny about that?"

"I don't know," said the private detective, "as there's anything funny about it. In fact it strikes me as kinda serious."

"Maybe you'll take a notion to mind your own damn business then, Mister."

"That's a thought at that," said Crole. "But if the D. A. sent you down here to watch me, maybe you'd better come up to my office. I can give you a drink and make you comfortable."

"Wise guy," said the man in the gray suit. "On your way. Know any more stories?"

"Yes," said Crole, "I do. That's a bright tie you have on. Too much color though for the work you're doing. It makes you conspicuous. Extend my regards to your boss." He turned away and had started towards the building's entrance when the man's abrupt: "Wait a second, Mister," caused him to pivot.

Crole had at different times seen the best of the old timers on the police force frisk men. But nothing he ever saw remotely approached the speed of this man's fingers and the deftness with which he got the paper-wrapped gun from the pocket of the private detective's coat.

The man with the purple tie hefted the package. "Gat," he said. "A .38 by the feel. Automatic. Got a permit?"

"Yes," said Crole. He realized that he had forgotten all about the gun. What he should have done was to have put it away in his office safe. He knew now that it was too late.

"Does the permit carry this gun's number?"

"No."

"All right. I'll keep this gun."

"I don't want you to do that," Crole said. "As it happens, I've got a legitimate reason for not wanting to lose it."

"If I showed you my shield, Crole, you'd shut up like a clam."

"There's something in that, too, I suppose—depending on the shield. Mind telling me who you are, or better yet, who you're working for? I'm one of them curious guys."

The man with the purple tie grinned for the first time. His eyes swerved to a spot beyond Crole's left shoulder. One of them seemed to twitch. "I'm curious, too, Crole. So much so that . . ."

"Mr. Crole," broke in a familiar voice in back of the private detective, "I've been looking all over for you."

Crole whirled. The eyes of the jaunty little man, August Fweeble, were beaming with pleasure. And the man's smile was like a benediction. Crole said: "Hello, Gus. I'm talking to a guy about . . ." He swung front again. "Hell! He's gone!"

"Who's gone? You mean that man in the gray suit? I saw him duck through the traffic just as you turned around."

Simon Crole blinked rapidly. He recalled the peculiar twitch in Purple Tie's eye a bare second before the sound of Fweeble's voice caused him to turn around. It was almost as if a signal had passed between the two men. "Gus," he said, eyeing the jaunty little man with the faintest trace of suspicion, "do I look like a hick?"

"You look all right to me. Why?"

"I just wondered. I feel as though somebody took me to the cleaner's, if you get what I mean. That man got away with something of mine. It wasn't mine exactly any more than it's his right now. And I can't figure out whether he was a city slicker, or a smooth dick from the prosecutor's office. I must be getting old."

"Was it something valuable?"

"I wish I knew myself," sighed Crole. "But I never had a chance to find out."

"The occurrence was unfortunate," said Fweeble, regretfully.

"Unfortunate doesn't quite fit the situation, Gus. I'm liable to be in jail within the next twenty-four hours."

"Surely it can't be that serious."

"You don't know how serious certain things can be unless you've tried to run a detective agency and keep people out of trouble."

August Fweeble waved trouble lightly aside. "I can't imagine a man of your ability in such a fix. All in your mind, Mr. Crole."

"Sure. That's just where I don't want it. It makes me nervous."

"I was up to your office a few minutes ago," said Fweeble, changing the subject, "and that—my, she's a pretty girl—and she said you were out."

"I was. I still am. Come back with me to that same office and I'll give you a drink."

"No thanks. I'm in somewhat of a hurry. What I wanted to tell you was that I got a card of admission to the Casino."

Crole regarded the little man with profound admiration. "You're good, Gus. How did you work it?"

"I obtained it from the portly gentleman named Schilling."

"Gus, are you kidding me? Why the Casino is owned by Schilling. It's one of the hardest places in town to get into. You must have considerable influence."

"A friend of mine introduced the subject to another friend. And this second friend introduced me to Mr. Schilling over at the Argus Club. It was really quite simple."

"I suppose it was," admitted Crole. "Then we'll go as planned Saturday night."

"That's why I came down to see you—to make certain you hadn't forgotten our engagement."

"I hadn't forgotten it," said Crole. "But I hadn't much hope of your being able to get a card of admission."

"It was really quite simple," beamed the jaunty little man, turning to leave. "Well, good night, Mr. Crole. I'll call for you . . ."

"At my office, Gus. Between nine and nine-thirty."

August Fweeble bowed and turned away. Crole stood for a moment at the curb watching the little man. He scratched his chin reflectively His eyes blinked rapidly. "There's something," he told himself, "odd about that gentleman. He knows where he's going. I wish the devil I did."

Moodily he returned to the building and went up to his office. Etta was dressed for the street. She regarded him reproachfully. "I thought you were coming right back."

"I thought so, too. But I run into a couple of guys." He looked at his watch. "Better go on home. It's after six. Anybody call while I was out?"

"Mr. Fweeble was in."

"I know. He was one of the guys I met downstairs."

"And Matt called. The furniture's come and he's got the new office nearly settled. And the men are putting in the phone."

"Swell. Run along, precious."

Etta gathered up the mail. Her eyes were serious. "Is everything all right?"

Simon Crole shoved both hands in his coat pockets. He smiled at her through half-closed eyes. "Everything's fine."

"You looked worried when you came in."

"Did I? You mistake worry for hunger pangs and the pleasures of the cup."

After the girl had left, Crole locked the hall door and went into his private office. He rolled a cigarette and smoked it with slow deliberation. Finished, he picked up the phone and called a number. "Herman," he said into the mouthpiece. "What's on the menu tonight? Fine. Roast chicken. Fruit salad. Rolls and a big pot of coffee. Yeah. Send it up to the office. I'm too busy to come down." He hung up.

His being busy consisted for the moment of leaning back in the swivel chair and elevating his feet to the desk. In this position he remained until he heard the elevator door clang. Then he got up and opened the door for the waiter.

"Anything else, Mr. Crole?" asked the man, setting the tray on the scarred desk.

Crole tipped him. "Nothing. Don't bother with the tray and dishes tonight. Pick them up in the morning."

The waiter nodded and went out the door.

Crole removed a folded napkin and laid it across his knee. He took the top from the dish of roasted chicken and removed therefrom a well-browned leg. His teeth bit into it just as the phone rang.

He took down the receiver. "Hello," he said.

"It's Matt," said the voice. "I'm in the new office. Room 613. The telephone number is Main 7218. The name on the door is THE TRI-CITY INVESTMENT CORPORATION. I figure that nobody would be looking for investments these days so we wouldn't be bothered with customers."

Still chewing on his chicken leg, Crole said, thickly: "What kind of a view have you got?"

"Not bad. It could be improved by having the building moved about six feet to the north. But we can see part of the office through one of the windows."

"A-huh."

"And I got two holes cut in the shade. I'll keep it three-quarters down. Then I can stand on a table out of line from the window and peek through without anybody across the street getting wise they're being watched."

"You grow more intelligent every day, Matt," observed Crole, gnawing from the bone in his fingers. "But don't make the mistake of letting O'Brien or anybody else of the organization see you going in and out of the building."

"There's a door to a side street that I'm using."

"Okay. I'll be down in the morning. G'bye." He hung up and reached for the coffee pot. A knock sounded on the hall door. "Damn!" he muttered, fervently.

He got up from his chair and went to the door. Opened it. Gordon Chadwick stood in the hall.

"Come in," invited Crole, keeping his amazement from showing.

Chadwick came in. His face was set in determined lines. He lit a cigarette and sat on the edge of a chair beside the private detective's desk.

"I'm glad you came," said Crole. "Save me a trip to Crown Beach."

"You knew, then, where . . ."

"It's my business to know, Chadwick. Excuse me while I go on with my supper. Go right ahead and get off your chest whatever's there. I'm listening."

He spread an opened roll with butter, laid a sizable chunk of chicken between the halves and popped it into his mouth. When next he glanced at his visitor he looked into the round bore of a .32 automatic.

He said nothing. He couldn't. His mouth was too full. Slowly he chewed, his unwavering eyes fixed on that little black hole that menaced him. Deliberately he stirred sugar into his coffee, swallowed, and found his voice.

"Seems to me I've seen you do this same thing before, Chadwick. It's bad business—for both of us. We won't get anywheres so long as you behave like this."

"Give me that pawn ticket you stole from my bathrobe. I've got to have it. If I don't get it . . ."

Crole swallowed his coffee and set the cup down. He buttered a second roll and inspected his fruit salad. "Put away the gun," he said.

"Give me what belongs to me."

"What makes you think I've got something of yours?"

"You were in my room, in my desk. You were hired by my father to find out all you could about me. You found the ticket in my bathrobe pocket. I want it, as I said before. If you don't give it to me—so help me God—I'll kill you."

Simon Crole munched unhappily on the buttered roll. "To be perfectly frank with you, Chadwick, I haven't got your ticket. I had it. I got the gun out of hock. But was hamstrung out of the weapon by an unfortunate circumstance quite beyond my control."

"You're lying. Mark Schilling's got your number. And so have I. Now I'm going to start counting. When I reach seven I'm going to pull the trigger, unless . . ." He paused.

"Unless what?"

"Unless you give me either the pawn ticket or the gun."

"You mean you'd actually shoot me?" Crole's eyes opened wide.

Chadwick's body was rigid. "One", he began. "Two . . ."

Crole poured himself a fresh cup of coffee.

"Three . . . four . . . five."

Crole lifted the cup to his lips. Then his wrist and arm snapped. The hot liquid shot across the desk and struck Chadwick squarely in the face. The gun jerked spasmodically. A bullet whipped past the lunging detective's cheek.

His arm crooked slightly as he rounded the desk corner. Then snapped outward and slightly upward. Clenched knuckles caught the boy on the right jaw. He fell back into the chair and slipped to the floor.

Crole rubbed his knuckles, picked the automatic from the floor and tossed it into a desk drawer. He lifted Chadwick's limp body from the floor and set him back into the chair.

The boy was out—out cold. Crole shook his head sadly. "Poor kid," he murmured. "He was so scared. And I hated like hell to get rough with him."

He returned to his chair behind the scarred desk and poured another cup of coffee. He drank it slowly and waited for the boy to recover.

Chadwick groaned after a time and started rubbing his jaw.

His eyes snapped open. They regarded Crole stupidly. But as memory returned, the stupidity changed to despair.

"I'm sorry I had to hit you, Chadwick," said Crole. "But I like to live as well as anybody else."

"You . . . you," faltered the boy. "You got my gun?"

"The last one—yes," observed Crole.

"What are you going to do?"

"Depends on you."

"Me?"

"Yes. You see, Gordon, believe it or not, I really want to help you. I'm not your enemy as you seem to think. I'm your friend."

"You . . . you're my friend," increduously. He leaned back in the chair. His lips twitched. A shudder passed over his body. Tears ran down his cheeks—tears of which he was not ashamed.

11

A NEWSPAPER CLUE

SIMON CROLE finished his supper slowly, and purposely kept his eyes from the troubled face of his visitor. He recognized, with cunning gained from long experience, that here was a boy who must be handled with extreme care.

He pushed the tray aside and rolled a cigarette. Got out his trick lighter and fumbled with it hopefully. It seldom worked. He found matches and lighted the cigarette.

Chadwick said: "Well, I guess I'll go."

"Don't. Not yet. Let's understand one another."

"It won't do any good I'm afraid. The evidence is too much. And now with the gun in the hands of the police . . ."

"Then it was Nicky's gun after all."

Chadwick nodded. "I found it in the car the next morning.

I was scared. I didn't want to throw it away where it would be found. And I was afraid to keep it in my room. So I pawned it."

"Chadwick," said Crole. "I didn't immediately depart from your house this afternoon when I left you in your room with your father and Mark Schilling. I went instead to the room adjoining your father's . . ."

Chadwick jumped to his feet. "You . . . you dared to go into the room that was once my moth . . .?"

"Easy, son," drawled Crole, "on that temper of yours. I went into your mother's room. But I didn't go there to search or to take anything. While in there I heard what you had to say to your father. Now tell me, what happened when you drove into the courtyard of the Green Gate?"

"You heard what I told my father . . ."

"Yes, yes. But you've left out certain things. Perhaps you don't realize you left them out. Perhaps you don't remember, as you stated. Now listen, and concentrate. We'll jog that memory of yours and see what happens. Sit back in your chair. Relax. Light a cigarette if it helps. Your life and the future career of your father depend on your answers."

Chadwick lighted a cigarette as Crole suggested and leaned back in his chair. "All right," he said. "I'll do the best I can to help you."

"That's fine. You and I'll get along together grand. Now. What was your connection with this Nicky Lombardo?"

"I met him through a girl I was friendly with at a night club. She said he was a big oil operator from Santa Fe Springs. We got friendly on drinks, and from drinks we went to poker."

"You found him a . . .?"

"He seemed regular enough, but queer. I couldn't make him out."

"You didn't know he was, well, a gangster of sorts?"

"I didn't know he was any different from what he said he was."

"What did you hope to gain from this man? I'd say he was definitely out of your class."

"He was. But I had it in the back of my mind to get into the oil business. I studied law against my own wishes. I was a failure. Everything I tried was no good. The oil business looked good to me. It seemed like a quick way of getting to the top. So I hung on to Nicky Lombardo."

"You hung on too long," said Crole, drily. "Now tell me some more. The night you drove Nicky to the Green Gate—was it for any particular purpose?"

Chadwick's forehead wrinkled with thought. "Yes. He was to meet a fellow there named . . . Ummm! I don't seem to remember."

"Was it O'Brien?"

"That's the man. How'd you guess it?"

"It doesn't matter. Did you ever hear Nicky mention any other names?"

"Yes. I remember one name in particular—Willie, it was."

"Willie who?"

"I never heard."

"Now when you've had too much liquor," Crole went on, "do you generally lose your memory like you did that night at the Green Gate? Understand, Gordon, you weren't asleep. You were very much awake when you drove that coupe of yours down the drive. I know. You almost ran over me."

"Something happens," said Chadwick. "No, I don't fall asleep. My mind and body keep on working, but my memory lags behind. I can't explain it any different."

"Did you know the cop was behind your car?"

"Nicky mentioned it once. But as I wasn't speeding I didn't pay much attention to what he said."

"You remember turning into the drive?"

"Vaguely."

"And nothing more, eh?"

"Nothing."

"Now wait a second. I'm going to reconstruct the scene. As your machine swung into the drive you hesitated for a moment, in doubt as to the best place to park. You backed up a couple of times then selected your place. Meantime the traffic officer had set his motorcycle on its standard and was coming towards your machine. Remember anything like that?"

"No. Nothing."

"Just about that time another car drove in. A sport roadster. It was driven by a man, a client of my agency. The lights of his car, as they curved along the driveway, suddenly illuminated the face of the motorcycle cop."

Chadwick closed his eyes. "I believe . . . I believe I do remember exactly that. The cop was in the glare of the roadster's headlights. He wasn't smiling. There was something hard and disagreeable in his face. His hand was close to a holster swinging on his hip."

"You take up from there."

"I can't. I don't remember."

"All right. Nicky began to squirm around on the seat beside you. Maybe he cursed."

"I still don't remember."

Crole's patience was exhaustless. "Then Malloy the traffic cop, came close to the car. He said something like this: 'All right, Nicky, get out and stick 'em up. You're wanted for the National' . . ."

Chadwick leaned suddenly forward and flung the cigarette on the floor. "He said 'Stick 'em up, Nicky. I got you cold. You're wanted down at Police Headquarters'." Chadwick's voice broke at this point. "Nicky's hand was suddenly in front of my face. And then the whole world seemed to explode. I saw the cop pitch sideways on his face. At the same time Nicky fell against my right shoulder. I gave him a shove. He toppled over and fell through the door to the running board. I started the motor. Nicky's body fell the rest of the way to the ground. I reached over and pulled the door shut. I . . . I guess that's all."

Beads of moisture were on the boy's forehead. He was trembling.

Simon Crole poured out a small glass from his choice Bourbon. "Here," he said. "This ought to straighten you out."

"No!" The refusal was firm. "Not while this business is hanging over my head."

"Good idea," approved Crole, neatly downing the contents of the glass. "Stick to it, Gordon, and you'll come out top side up."

He returned bottle and glass to the desk drawer and smiled his surprised smile on the trembling boy. "Don't worry. I didn't think you killed the cop. But I had to be positive."

"Suppose I went to the police and told . . ."

"If you did," said Crole, no longer smiling, "it would be

just too bad. Don't forget Nicky's statement as to who did the killing. His word, even though he is dead, is as good as yours. And remember, Mark Schilling holds a big club over your father. Furthermore, if he knew that you had been in to see me, he wouldn't hesitate to give you the works—and it would be plenty tough."

"I'll do whatever you say."

"Fine. All I ask of you is to disappear. Fade. Vanish from the picture. I'm not certain yet where that gun of Lombardo's is. If the police have it, as I hope they haven't, I'll be hauled up on the carpet in the district attorney's office pronto."

Chadwick got to his feet. He looked at his watch. "It's almost nine. Just got time to catch the Pacific Electric for the beach. You'll . . . you'll keep in touch with me, Mr. Crole, in case . . ."

"When I want you Gordon," said Crole, "I'll contact you at the Crown Beach post office either at noon or six o'clock at night. Clear?"

Chadwick nodded and pulled on his hat. "I feel better already. If you see Dad, you'll tell him, of course. Tell him I'll be all right and not to worry."

"I'll tell him," said Crole, which was a forthright lie, for he had no intention of contacting Judge Benson Chadwick. "Luck, boy. And keep out of sight."

For some time after young Chadwick had left, Simon Crole sat impassively behind his desk. The cold remains of the supper finally got him down. He left his desk and went to the window. From below the raucous bellowing of newspaper vendors floated up. He turned from the window. Found an old rag and mopped up the spilled coffee from the floor. He dropped the rag in the waste basket and examined the broken plaster on the wall where a bullet lay imbedded—the bullet that had passed so close to his cheek.

He sat down again and rubbed his bald head. He thought of Biff Larkin, calmly taking his sentence of ten years without squealing on his pal. Some guys could take it. Larkin was one of that type.

He thought of Nicky Lombardo stretched out on a cold slab at the morgue, drilled by a cop's bullet. He thought of Officer Malloy. What started Malloy on the trail of Nicky? No good.

He couldn't get into Malloy's mind, for the motorcycle cop was also out of the picture.

From his desk drawer he removed the photostatic copy of the statement so damning to Gordon Chadwick. He studied it with some care—not so much the words but the character of the type. It was obvious that the thing wasn't written in the hospital. Someone who knew Nicky Lombardo, had written it. Nicky must have been too far gone to realize what he had signed. And Mark Schilling was planning to use this statement as an extortion club.

This was quite simple and perfectly obvious. But what connection did all this have with the death of Jensen the cashier?

He took out his notebook and jotted down: "Check Nicky's statement with type on fat man's correspondence. Check Jensen's financial standing." He closed the book, pocketed it, picked up his hat and yawned.

For some minutes he stood in front of the window, staring down into the street, listening to the pulse beat of the city street. The office seemed suddenly a place he wanted to get out of. He put on his hat, switched off the lights and went out to the elevator.

He bought the late edition of the *Ledger* from a middle-aged newsboy, tucked it under his arm and went into a coffee shop around the corner. While he waited for coffee to cool he unfolded the paper and scanned the headlines.

A sly grin spread over the private detective's face as he read. Farrel, the city editor, had taken the questions Crole had phoned in, twisted them, turned them inside out, improved upon them and had scattered them all over the first two pages.

By suggestion, by innuendo, the editor dragged the city administration and the police over the hot coals of public criticism.

"Our city is the finest in the west," ran the lead paragraph. *"Our leaders are efficient, honest and mindful of the public weal. But are they as efficient, honest and as zealous of public needs as they should be? Thoughtful readers should think this over."*

Crole turned to the second page and read! *"We call our police the 'finest' which they are. They are courageous, clean and remarkably efficient. Yet certain crime continues to stalk the streets of our city. Men, women and children are shot down ruthlessly. Is it the fault of the police? We don't like to think so. But crime is not being stamped out. Who is at fault?"*

And also: *"Of the two hundred thousand dollars taken from the National City, only thirty-five thousand was recovered by our police. This will mean nothing to you, Mr. Average Reader. You won't have to pay the loss. But somebody will. A vicious gunman named Larkin has just been sent to prison for his part in the hold-up."*

Crole sighed and continued reading: *"He admitted taking thirty-five thousand. But who got the rest of this colossal sum? A hundred and sixty-five thousand dollars is still unaccounted for. Somebody has it. The duty of our police is plain. They must find the guilty ones and bring them to justice."*

Down in the corner of the second sheet was a small head-line: *"Was Cashier Jensen murdered? Police are unable to determine whether his death was a suicide, or the work of a rope fiend."*

Crole turned over another page and found it covered with a full page of news photos. Among them was one that was not a picture of world celebrities, but of a group of rather startled people in front of the National City Bank.

The picture was dark in spots where the printing ink had smeared. Crole read the explanatory line below it: *"One minute after the robbery."*

The faces of the men and women running towards the bank were slightly blurred. The angle from which the picture was taken must have been the opposite corner across the main street. The view showed a side street as well as the main one.

Coming down the main street was a police car with two cops standing on the running board. But of the robbers, there was no sign.

In picking out the details in his usually meticulous way, Simon Crole made an important discovery. He blinked at what he saw, pursed his lips and examined the pictured object closer . . .

"A newspaper clue," he muttered to himself. "Now what do you think of that?" Abruptly he folded the paper, finished his coffee and went out into the street.

. Within five minutes he was inside the *Ledger* office. He

smiled pleasantly at a girl behind the railing in the front office. "I want to talk with one of your photographers, Harry Spraker."

Spraker came into the office and recognized the private detective. "Hello, Crole. What's on your mind."

Crole led him outside. "How'd you like to pick up a piece of change, Harry?"

"It all depends."

"Say twenty-five bucks."

"Sounds okay. What's the racket?"

"No racket, Harry. Just a favor. There's a picture in your late edition taken immediately after that bank robbery. I want the use of the negative plate."

"I was the guy who took that picture, Crole, but the plate is not my property."

"Sure. I'm not asking you to give it to me. All I want is the loan of it for a couple hours. When I've finished, I'll bring it back. Get me the plate, Harry, and the twenty-five is yours."

"Wait around the corner of the building," said Spraker. "I'll be with you in ten minutes."

In ten minutes he was there with the plate wrapped in a newspaper. "Don't forget to get it back, Crole. I'm risking my job to do this for you."

"Sure. I may want your help again. I won't let you down, Harry. Here's for the favor." He shoved three folded bills into Spraker's palm and went down the street.

He looked at his watch. Ten o'clock. He scowled, then went into a drugstore and called a number on the telephone.

"Hello, Don," he said to the voice that answered. "You still up? Listen, I've got a negative that I want printed. Also an enlargement made of it. I can only have use of the plate for a couple hours. Can you do it for me in that time? You can? Good. I'll be up to your house pronto."

It was close to eleven when Crole got back to the *Ledger* office with the plate. He returned it to Spraker, and with the still damp enlargement that the photographer had made tucked under his arm, he got into a taxi and was driven to his apartment.

There was a closed car out in front that looked strangely familiar. Crole eyed it biliously. He went into the building,

Captain Jorgens was sitting in the foyer, his teeth clamped pugnaciously on the end of a black cigar.

He got up as the private detective came in. " 'Lo, Simon," he said.

Simon Crole nodded. "How are you, Captain." Then to the young woman behind the switchboard, "Any calls for me, dear?"

"None, Mr. Crole."

Crole thanked her and turned towards the police officer. "Been waiting long, Captain?"

"Over an hour."

"Do you good to wait," observed Crole, leading the way upstairs to his apartment. "You've left me to cool my heels outside your office more than once—sometimes out of pure spite."

Captain Jorgens said nothing till the door of the apartment clicked shut, then he exploded rather violently. "Simon, damn you," he snapped. "The time is coming when I'm going to throttle you with these here fingers." He held out two big paws.

Crole regarded them mildly. "First, Captain, we'll have a drink. I'm in no condition to talk until . . ."

"All right, all right! Pour the drinks and get it over with. Then, by God, you're going to do considerable talking, or the Simon Crole detective agency is going to be folded up like a flat pocketbook and dumped into an ash can."

The scar on Simon Crole's Buddha-like face twisted his lips into their smile of perpetual surprise. He made a ticking sound with his lips. "Tsk, tsk, Captain. Don't be that way. From the manner in which you consigned me to the ash can, I gather, in my slow way, that you're mad at me."

"Damn right I'm mad," exploded the police officer. "And sore!"

12

SIMON CROLE set his empty glass on a table and rolled a cigarette. Inhaling deeply he said: "It's past my usual time for retirement, Captain. And I'm one of those individuals who need plenty of sleep."

"You ever tried sleeping on one of our cots with iron springs, Simon? That's an experience that's not altogether impossible of realization."

"Sounds like a threat."

"Take it any way you want to."

"I'd prefer to think about something pleasanter—say another drink."

"Simon, I see you have a folded copy of tonight's *Ledger* in your pocket. You've read it, of course."

"Every line. I'm a voracious reader, Captain."

"And you noticed, perhaps, Editor Farrel's delicate technique of calling the police a bunch of bums."

"As an average reader, Captain, it started me to thinking."

"Rot! Listen here, Simon. Somebody called Editor Farrel on the phone and asked him these questions. I found that out. But I couldn't find out who called him I don't know as it makes any difference. My own feeling in the matter is this: You shouldn't have done it, Simon. It means a shake-up on the force."

Crole blinked. "You think I called Farrel and suggested these things to him?"

"Think!" snorted Jorgens. "I know damned well you did. I recognize your touch, your method. No one else could have done it."

"Maybe you're right, Captain," admitted Crole. "But if I did call Farrel, I called him for a reason."

"Now we're getting somewheres. Why did you tip off Farrel?"

"To help the police."

Jorgens laughed harshly. "Tripe, Simon, and you know it."

"It was my idea to stir the police into activity," said Crole. "But I did not intend a wholesale shake-up."

"Well, maybe not. But you stirred things up. Not only in the Commissioner's office, but outside as well. A dozen organizations have called headquarters and asked why something isn't done to curb this wave of lawlessness sweeping over our fair city. Even the Federals are beginning to ask 'how come'."

"Are the G-men in on this?" asked Crole.

"No. Why should they be?"

"I just wondered," said Crole. He unrolled the enlargement of the picture appearing in the *Ledger* and spread it out on the table. "Captain, there's something I want, and can't get. But you can get it for me without arousing suspicion."

The police officer scowled. "There's trickery involved," he said. "I can smell it."

"Merely an exchange. What I want is an architect's plan of the fifth floor of the Commerce building, with the names of the lessees of all the offices."

Jorgen's lidded eyes began to close. "Simon, do you realize what you're asking?"

Crole nodded. "You're not afraid of Mark Schilling, are you?"

"Afraid? Listen, Simon, what's in the back of your head? I don't want to do anything to antagonize Schilling. He's a big stick in this city. He can make it tough for me if he wants to."

"Your hands are clean, aren't they?"

"You know damn well they are."

"Then why the apprehension?"

Captain Jorgens jerked the cigar from between his teeth. "Simon, how many ops have you on your payroll?"

"Two right now. Generally one."

"Loyal?"

"Absolutely."

"Suppose you had a great many operators. Suppose one of them was disloyal?"

"I'd kick him out."

"And suppose you didn't know who to kick out?"

Simon Crole blinked and said nothing.

Jorgens smiled thinly. "Exactly. I don't know myself. I merely suspect. There are leaks in my office. And there's nothing I can do about them. Any move I make where Mark Schilling is involved will be reported to him within an hour after I make it."

"Isn't there someone on the D.A.'s staff whom you could trust?"

"The men on the district attorney's staff are *his* men, not mine. We can cooperate in the handling of ordinary criminal matters. But on matters involving Mark Schilling—well, that's entirely different. If Schilling ever found out that the fifth floor of the Commerce building was being checked, whoever was doing the checking would be without a job in twenty-four hours. He's that powerful."

"I see. Well, think it over, Captain. You must have one man. Someone you can trust. You needn't promise a thing. Now listen, I'm going to give you a tip."

"Go ahead."

"The man who helped Larkin on the National City job was Nicky Lombardo. Wait. You needn't take my word for it. Get a picture of him and show it to any of the witnesses. Another thing. Officer Malloy knew Nicky was the other man. Malloy was trailing him the night both men shot it out at the Green Gate."

"You sure that Malloy knew . . ."

"Here," said Crole, "is an enlargement of a picture taken by one of the *Ledger* men. It's a clearer piece of work than the print in the newspaper. And it was taken one minute after the hold-up. It shows the arrival of the police."

Jorgens squinted at the picture. "I was in that car coming down the street. Ours was the first machine to arrive. But Malloy wasn't with me. So how could he have known . . ."

"A slight detail in the lower right hand corner of the picture, Captain. See it? The rear end of a police motorcycle. Below the red glass of the tail-light is a license plate bearing the number X-309, which you will find on checking belongs, or did belong, to Officer Malloy."

"Well?" frowned the police officer. "What of it?"

"Just this, Captain. It proves that Malloy was on the scene of the bank hold-up before you were, since his machine is already parked at the curb. And if he was there before you got to the bank, it's not impossible to believe that he saw the faces of the robbers as they lammed from the scene in their get-away car. Malloy knew all the time who the second man was, and was planning to make the pinch by himself so as to get full credit. Well, he failed."

"It sounds like Malloy," admitted Jorgens, grudgingly. "He was like that—always playing a lone hand. I admire his nerve, but he showed poor judgment. You're giving me this picture, aren't you?"

"If you'll forget where it came from."

"I've forgotten already," said the police officer, rising to his feet, and thrusting the rolled picture into his pocket. "I won't use this information right now, or even make it known among my men. I'll save it. Maybe I can get more use out of it that way."

Crole's smile was enigmatic. "There are times, Captain, when your mind works brilliantly."

Jorgen's eyebrows arched deceptively. "You're deep, Simon, too deep for a square-toed dick like me. All right. Just what did you mean by that last crack?"

"I meant that you're learning, Captain."

"Learning what?"

"How to keep your bright boys busy, and at the same time not letting them in on everything you know. That's one way to stop leaks."

Jorgens grunted. "Heard anything new on the Jensen case?"

"Haven't given it much thought—lately."

"Is Schilling mixed up in it?"

"I wouldn't know. Honestly."

"You missed your calling, Simon. You should have been a horse thief instead of a private dick."

"Meaning I'm a liar?"

"Bluntly—yes."

Simon Crole grinned placidly. "If I didn't like you, Captain, I'd tell you to go to hell."

"I'm relieved, Simon. Are you hired by Jensen's estate, or . . . ?"

"No."

"Wait till I've finished. Or are you working for the National City?"

"Neither," said Crole, yawning. "Wrong, both guesses."

Jorgens extended his hand. "Good night, Simon. I get sleepy the same as you do. And I go on duty at six. We still good friends?"

"As good as we'll ever be."

"You know my number. If you get in a jam . . ."

"I don't expect to, but I'll keep you in mind just in case." He turned to the bottle on the table. "Have a nightcap before you go?"

The police officer growled something unintelligible and went out of the apartment.

"Ummm!" grunted Simon Crole, unfastening his necktie. "If I succeeded in stirring up the police, I must have reached others as well. Tomorrow I'll know for sure—if I am not bumped off."

Nonchalantly, at nine the next morning, he strolled into his office. "Precious," he asked, dropping into a chair beside his secretary's desk, "what is today?"

Etta smiled rosily. "Payday. And now is as good a time as any to speak about that raise you promised me."

Crole's eyebrows went up. "Didn't I give you that raise?"

"You promised it, but you did not authorize it."

"I authorize it now. How much?"

"Ummm. Let me see."

"Never mind. Five bucks more each week. Not a nickel more."

"Boss, you're swell!"

Simon Crole was secretly pleased. But he did not show it. "What day is today?" he asked again.

"Saturday."

"Saturday. I have an appointment with one of my clients, Mr. August Fweeble. We're going to Mark Schilling's Casino. Somewhere in my apartment I've got a dress suit . . ."

"I'll take care of everything. What time you going?"

"Sometime after nine tonight."

"Everything will be laid out when you go home after supper."

Crole got to his feet. "And lay me out some money, too. I got about ten bucks. I'll need a couple hundred."

He left her desk and went into his private office. He closed the door. Went over to his desk. Pawed around it for a while. Went into the washroom. Turned on bother taps. Turned them off. Looked at himself in a mirror, shook his head sadly, and returned to his desk, upon which he presently placed both feet.

He took a notebook from his pocket. Opened it and read; "Check Nicky's statement with type on the fat man's correspondence. Check Jensen's financial standing."

The financial rating of Jensen required delicate handling. He'd turn that over to Esther to solve. But trying to check the type on Mark Schilling's correspondence was something he must attend to himself.

The telephone rang. It was his operator Matt Ridley. "Hello, Boss," said Ridley. "The set-up is complete. It ain't quite as hot though, as I thought it'd be. They's steel shutters on the fat guy's windows like Venetian blinds. And they're pulled down about half way of the window length."

Crole said: "Any activity there this morning?"

"Nothing. I don't think that the big boy is down yet."

"Well, keep your eye on the street entrance as well as the window. If you see any eggs that look tough like O'Brien and that bunch, watch to see if they go into Mark's office. Esther there? Put her on the wire."

The contralto voice of his new operator came over the wire. "Yes, Simon."

"Yes, what? I ain't said anything yet. Listen. You're a lawyer, or you're going to be one. So you must be smart. Now I got a lawyer's job for you."

"It *would* be. Today is Saturday. You asked me to keep this evening open. What are you planning?"

"That's right," said Crole. "Be down at the office at nine. We're stepping out with—you remember Gus Fweeble? Well, Gus is taking us to the Casino—the swellest gambling joint in town."

"I was going to bet on the races at Santa Anita this afternoon . . ."

"Save your money 'till tonight. Then you can lose it in a big way. Now listen. Here's what I want. You remember that cashier of the National City who was supposed to have committed suicide the other day? Well, I want a financial report on him. Find out if possible if he used any big sums of money just prior to his death. And don't let on to anybody that you're working for me." •

"You realize," said Esther, "that the police . . ."

"Sure. I know. They'd be dumb if they hadn't already checked Jensen's money transactions. That's what I meant by the ticklish part. But do the best you can. Banks and brokers' offices close at twelve so you won't have much time. Hop to it. I'll see you later. Send Matt back to the phone."

"Yeah," said Matt, after a moment.

"Matt," said Crole. "I'm calling on Mark Schilling in about fifteen minutes. What I've got in my mind may not pan out. If I think it will, I'll get as near the window as possible and stand with my back to it. If you see me holding my hat against the back of my knees, you'll know I want you to tail somebody that will shortly leave the building. I don't know who it will be, but he will probably be carrying a bulky package under his arm."

"Sure. I get the idea."

"Matt, I want to get hold of that package. I don't care how you get it—but get it!"

"Leave it to me. I'll get down to the street the moment I get the hat signal."

"Swell, but don't pay any attention to me when I come out. Keep your eyes wide open for the gent with the package."

"Right."

Simon Crole hung up. He went to the outer office. "Precious," he said, "I'm calling on Mark Schilling."

Etta's eyes were startled for a moment. "Be careful, boss. I'm afraid of that man. He's got too much power."

The fanwise wrinkles radiating from the corners of the private detective's eyes deepened. He smiled heavily. "That's the very reason I'm going to see him. He's got too much power."

"He's cunning."

"So I've heard."

"And ruthless."

The heavy smile continued. "Don't worry your pretty head about Simon. You stay here and take care of the fort and don't let any yeggs walk off with our safe. Bye." He bowed, clapped on his hat, and went out.

The sallow-faced man at the eyepiece of the periscopic arrangement spoke into the mouthpiece of the inter-office phone to the fat man in the front office.

"They's a big guy just come out of the elevator," he said. "Looks like a dick. He's coming down the hall now, looking around. Walking slow and taking in everything in sight. New face. Don't belong to the Headquarters crowd."

"All right," said the fat man, returning the receiver to its hook.

His pale eyes widened as he contemplated the possible significance of what might be on his caller's mind. Aside from the widening of the eyes, his ponderous face showed no signs of the faint perturbation that pulsed through the gross hulk of his body.

The hall door swung inward. Crole stepped into a reception office.

Marie's steel-trap mouth formed two words. "Good morning."

Crole mentally catalogued her face with a single glance. He nodded pleasantly. "Mr. Schilling in?"

"I'll see. Who shall I tell him . . ."

"Simon Crole, sister."

"Did you have an appointment?"

Crole shook his head. "No."

A buzzer beneath the girl's desk sounded a double note which Crole interpreted as coming directly from Schilling who knew in advance of his arrival.

"Mr. Schilling will see you," said the steel-trap mouth. "Straight ahead through the door."

Simon Crole went through the door. The feeling that he had been observed the moment he left the elevator crystallized into a cold fact. He wondered how and by what means this had been accomplished.

As he passed into the inner sanctum of the city's political boss, he became aware of a splendor that put his own shabby office to shame. Panel woodwork, oil paintings, thick rugs and costly furniture.

He noticed these things only in passing. Whatever he saw, thought or felt, left no trace on his Buddha-like face. In this respect he and Mark Schilling were evenly matched. He came to a stop before the desk of the fat man, feet spread wide apart. The silence of the room was brooding, fetid. The eyes of both men met, clashed and held steady.

Behind the pale blue orbs of Mark Schilling was mockery and thinly disguised contempt.

But the gray eyes of Simon Crole were like chunks of frozen fog—and quite as unfathomable.

Crole said blandly: "How are you, Schilling?"

The puffy lips of the fat man scarcely moved. "What brings you here, Crole? I don't recall that we have any business with each other."

"Possibly not, Schilling. But we have."

"So? And the nature of this business?"

"Greed, I suppose," Crole said. "Greed for money—the curse of our present civilization. Also a slight peeve, Schilling, that needs to be corrected."

13

A HOT MACHINE

MARK SCHILLING grunted from behind his desk. "Hmmm! Sit down."

Simon Crole eased his body into a chair. His eyes moved restlessly around the room as if he were seeing the splendor of the office for the first time. "Grand place you've got here," he approved. "That Rembrandt on the south wall is a priceless thing in itself. Must take a sizable quantity of our present day currency to keep up a place like this."

"Think so?"

"A-huh. Mind if I roll a cigarette? I'm a low-brow in some of my habits." Deftly he rolled a cigarette, popped it between his lips and lit it. "Too bad about that fellow Jensen," he went on, exhaling with the same breath. "Believe me, Schilling, that man never hung himself like the papers said he did. Not him. He was too well heeled. Somebody else fastened that rope around his neck."

"Think so?"

"Don't you ever read the papers?"

"Seldom."

"Didn't anybody tell you about what was in the *Ledger* last night about the Jensen case—how they was still a hundred and sixty-five grand missing from the bank vault?"

"Things of this nature do not concern me."

Crole realized suddenly that his agitation of the public press had failed of its purpose. Schilling refused to be stampeded into showing his hand. Well, he'd try another line.

"The police down at Headquarters think maybe I had a hand in bumping off Jensen."

Schilling smiled pityingly. His chair creaked as he leaned back. "I'm not the least bit interested in the Jensen case. You came here with something else on your mind. Get it over with. I'm busy."

"I was getting around to it in my own clumsy way, Schilling. What I come to see you about is Judge Chadwick."

Schilling's lips puffed out, and he scratched the rolls of fat beneath his chin. "What about Chadwick?"

"That's what I'm here for. To find out."

"You've come to the wrong place."

"I don't think so."

Schilling tapped the desk top with pudgy fingers. "I don't know anything about the arrangement between you and the judge, Crole, but I do remember distinctly that he dismissed you from the case. Am I right?"

Crole nodded, "You're right."

"So what?"

"He dismissed me," said Crole, "because you interfered. I had him sewed up. My fee was to have been five thousand. You butted in. I'm canned. And all I get out of the case is a measly five hundred."

"That's your hard luck."

"Maybe it is. But that don't close up the case, Schilling."

"No?"

Crole wagged his head slowly. "Nope. It doesn't close the case at all. I'm still thinking about that forty-five hundred bucks I would have gotten if you hadn't busted into the picture. Does that suggest anything to you?"

The eyelids of the fat man began to droop. "It suggests a form of blackmail, Crole."

"Then you misunderstood me. All that I suggested was that I'm out the biggest part of a fee I would have collected from the judge if someone hadn't interfered and spoiled a legitimate business transaction."

"There's a distinction in what you suggested, but it's no different from what you inferred. What do you expect me to do—start crying?"

"No," said Crole, wagging his head. "I expect you to start shelling out."

The contempt was gone from Schilling's pale eyes. In its place was something that was not pleasant. "You've got a lot of gall, Crole—coming to me with such an idea in your mind."

"Forty-five hundred is what I've got coming," said Crole, mildly, "and forty-five hundred is what I expect to get."

"Has it occurred to you, Crole, that the sum of four thousand five hundred dollars means as much to me as it does to you?"

"If it did, I don't remember it."

"Have you seen Judge Chadwick and wept on his shoulder?"

Simon Crole rubbed his bald head. "Schilling, you're good. The hell with the judge. I'm washed up with that bird. I sent him a bill for five-hundred, and I'll be lucky to get that much. What did I do to earn it? Nothing. I read a statement supposed to have been signed by some guy named Nicky Lombardo."

"Yes," said the fat man, tapping his desk lightly. "Go on."

"This Nicky," resumed Crole, "remarks among other things that the judge's son, Gordon, bumped off a motorcycle cop. It don't sound reasonable to me. So I goes to talk with the kid. And what do I find out? Ask me, Schilling. Just as I get the kid backed into a corner in comes the judge himself, and you. And I get canned."

"Sure. Why not?"

"I wish I knew. Forty-five hundred bucks is a neat sum any way you look at it. And I don't like to see it get through my fingers without grabbing at it. I tries to locate the kid. But he must have been scared out. I can't trace him."

Schilling's voice was silken smooth. "What became of the document you mentioned?"

"Oh, that! It wasn't a document. It was a photostatic copy of a document. I got it in my office somewhere. But that ain't the point, Schilling. Do I get my money?"

The fat man smiled unpleasantly. "Not from me."

"That's all right, too. I really didn't expect you'd see the case from my angle. Well," He got to his feet slowly. "I guess I'll amble down to the district attorney's office and turn the whole thing over to him. I'm damned sick of being made a goat of."

Schilling said quietly: "This photostatic copy you have, Crole. I'd like to see it."

"Hell," exploded the private detective. "It come from you in the first place. Judge Chadwick said you gave it to him."

"That's right. I gave it to him without examining it very closely. It came to me through the mail."

"No," said Crole, shaking his head doubtfully. "I wouldn't want to do that. I'll turn it over to Minifie and let him do the worrying. It's a good photostatic copy. The typewriter characters are plain. Maybe he can ferret out the machine used to type it."

He paused. Examined the leather binding in his hat, then let his arm drop loosely behind his back so that the hat was behind his knees. "All I'll tell Minifie is this: Somebody sent it to Schilling. Schilling gave it to the judge. And the judge passed it on to me. None of us know anything about it. And Nicky, who might have known, is dead."

"It won't work," said the fat man, leaning forward. "I'll tell you why. Judge Chadwick, I am sure, would pay you the forty-five hundred dollars you demand rather than risk public exposure of his son. Maybe the boy is guilty. Maybe he isn't."

"I ain't caring one way or the other," scowled Crole. "Either I get my forty-five hundred, or the photostatic copy of the statement goes to Minifie. Hell, that type would be easy to trace.

There's an 'e' with its horizontal line broken in the center. There's three or more cockeyed letters. Also the capital 'N' used in Nicky and Nurse is way below the letters that follow it. I ain't no expert, but I could pick out that machine in less than a minute—providing I could get around like the police can."

"Interesting," drawled the fat man. "Very. Suppose, Crole, you do nothing about this matter for the present. It may be just possible that I can make Judge Chadwick see things your way. If the judge refuses, you've lost nothing. Because you can't lose anything you've never really had."

"I just as good as had that five thousand," complained Crole. "I figured it was in the bank. Well, I'll hold off till Monday. But if he doesn't come through by then, Minifie get's the little picture of Nicky's statement, and he can start checking up typewriters. And if he wants to begin at my office and look my wreck over, that's okay with me." He put on his hat. "See you Monday, Schilling."

The fat man nodded, but did not get up. Hardly had he received the signal from the lookout that Crole had passed into the elevator, when he pressed a button.

The panel leading to the contractor's office opened. Gat O'Brien, hands in his coat pocket, stepped through the opening.

"Marie's machine," said Schilling. "It's hot. Take it out of the office. Wrap it up well and get rid of it. Drop it into the river, or the ocean. But get it out of here just about as fast as you can. Get it from Marie and bring it in here first."

O'Brien, slightly puzzled did as he was ordered. He set the machine on Schilling's desk.

The fat man looked it over. "L. C. Smith, model 8 with a ten inch carriage. Get another of the same description at a typewriter place. And you needn't say who it's for. Just get it and bring it in. Marie will pay you for whatever it costs."

"You want me," asked O'Brien, still puzzled, "to swap this in for another just like it?"

"No. I want this one destroyed, burned up, dropped into hell or the Pacific ocean. Is that clear?"

O'Brien nodded. "Okay. I'll get rid of it and bring back another just like it."

He lifted it from the desk and carried it into the contractor's office where he carefully bundled it into heavy drafting paper and fastened it with twine.

This done, he went out into the hall and took the elevator to the street.

Gat O'Brien was not heavily endowed with brains. True, he made an excellent body-guard, had more than his share of courage and was faithful to the man he served. But he was also, and this is no fault of his, entirely ignorant of why Schilling had ordered this machine taken from his office and destroyed.

Nor could it be said with complete fairness that O'Brien was shiftless or lazy. The river was at the other end of town, a long distance away, and was probably dried up. The ocean was still farther away. There was no way he could figure out how he could possibly drop it into hell, as Schilling had suggested.

So he did the first thing that came to his mind. He took it to a man who bought used guns, typewriters, trick jewelry and the like, and disposed of it for eleven dollars with no questions asked.

He pocketed the eleven, went to a place called Little Chicago and had a few drinks. He talked with some cronies, ate a leisurely lunch and again went out to the streets.

Shortly thereafter, he purchased a second machine, same make and model as the first, and returned to the Commerce building slightly bored with his morning's work, but eleven dollars richer.

During the time O'Brien was eating his leisurely lunch, Matt Ridley was haggling over the preposterous price of fifteen dollars he was asked to pay for the possession of a typewriter.

Matt scratched his head. "All right," he finally told the dealer. "I'll give you fifteen dollars for the machine. But if they's anything haywire with it, back it comes."

"This machine," explained the dealer, confidentially, pleased with the quick turnover on his eleven dollar investment, "has just been adjusted and overhauled. Honest, I ain't kidding you. I guarantee it absolutely for a whole year."

"Fair enough," said Ridley. "Now, since this typewriter is for the company which I work, I got to have a receipt showing how much I paid for it and the date. Also," he watched the dealer complete the bill of sale. "Also put down the serial number. It's on the casting in the back."

He checked the factory serial number with his receipt, paid over the fifteen dollars and walked out of the shop with the machine under his arm. He entered his own building from the street side, and went up in the elevator just as O'Brien turned into the entrance of the Commerce building carrying a new machine.

Matt set the typewriter on the floor while he unlocked the door. Esther was out. He closed the door and placed the newly acquired typewriter on a desk. Being quite as ignorant as O'Brien of the latent possibilities of his purchase, Ridley gave it no more thought. The important thing, at the moment, was to watch the office across the street.

Schilling's office, when Matt returned to the two peep-holes he had cut in the window shade, was apparently empty. Since his range of vision was limited because of the angle of the two windows, he could not see the entire office. Consequently, he failed to see the fat man press a button that worked the wall panel.

But he did see the panel open and O'Brien step through the wall opening, carrying what looked like another typewriter. "Holy cats!" gasped Ridley, unable to believe what he had seen. "O'Brien walks right through the wall."

He could not guess the cause of what happened next. One minute O'Brien was standing in the middle of the room facing somebody out of sight. The next he had jumped back through the panel and disappeared. But if Ridley failed to guess the cause of O'Brien's precipitous retreat, he was only too well aware of the effect.

O'Brien was in a sudden yank to go places. Ridley saw him race out of the front entrance a few moments later.

Matt Ridley yawned. "O'Brien must be going to the races," he told himself aloud, "or . . ."

He rubbed his nose. It occurred to him that it was too early for the races, that O'Brien had something else on his troubled mind, and that something else was not nags, but a certain typewriter he had so foolishly disposed of. Matt whistled softly.

At that moment there was a fumbling at the lock of the door. Esther Manning came in. "Matt," she said, throwing herself into a chair and lighting a cigarette. "You look like a Peeping Tom. Do you see anything? Have you seen anything? Or are you just looking?"

"Yes, to all three. I saw a guy carrying a typewriter walk through a solid wall that swung back. I saw him get excited and beat it back through said wall. Then come out of the building on the run."

"The reason for all this escapes me," said Esther, sententiously. "I've grown stale working for the County. If I ever had any cunning, I have it no longer. The morning is gone and I haven't accomplished a thing. Simon will be disappointed."

Matt said from his position at the peepholes. "They ain't nobody in sight. The big guy must be at his desk, but I can't see him. I wish this window was six feet up the street."

"Always wanting something you haven't got," remarked Esther. "I'm going to call Simon and tell him . . ."

"Listen," called Matt from the window. "That typewriter on the desk came from Mark Schilling's office. Gat O'Brien sold it to a second-hand dealer. I bought it up. Paid fifteen bucks for it."

Esther examined her pink nails. And from her nails her eyes strayed to an exquisitely wrought bracelet of carved links. Dangling to the bracelet, where it might easily become caught on something and be torn off, was a gold key.

She had never told Matt Ridley what this key signified. In a way she was proud of it. There weren't many of these keys being handed out. Just a few for the entire country. That key meant that Esther Manning had attained an unusually high ranking when she graduated from law school.

The expression in her eyes as she looked at the golden key was anything but brilliant. Little wrinkles formed between her eyes. "Matt" she said, "What do you know about cashier Charles Jensen?"

"I know he's dead. How come he died, I don't know. I got a good suspicion that the boss knows. That's why he sent you out—to prove his suspicions. I guess you found out plenty, hey?"

"Nothing. Somebody went over the ground before me and took everything away. Somebody . . ."

There was a gentle tap on the door.

"See who it is," said Matt, "and tell him the firm's manager is out. Gone home. Tell him . . ."

Esther opened the door. The wrinkles from between her eyes smoothed out. She smiled. "In, Simon," she said, opening the door. "I want to make a confession."

"A confession?" Simon Crole took one of her hands between his own and patted it lightly. "You ran into difficulties. I'm not surprised, but I had to be certain."

Esther eyed him sadly. "And you sent me out, knowing in advance that I wouldn't get anywhere?"

"I knew nothing, dear. I merely suspicioned certain things. Don't be concerned with your failure. I'm not." He turned to his operator behind the window.

"Matt," he said. "I see we've acquired a typewriter."

"Yeah, Boss. I followed the guy when he came out of the building carrying a bundle as you thought he would. He went to a dealer five blocks away who handles odd things. I waits till he leaves then goes in. The dealer was just putting the machine on a shelf. I negotiates for it, and he knocks it down to me for fifteen bucks."

"Fifteen bucks, eh?" Crole found a sheet of paper and rolled it into the machine. He typed a sentence with two fingers, took the paper close to the window and examined what he had written.

"A swell investment, Matt. I think I can sell the machine back to the original owner for maybe five thousand. And after I've completed that sale, I can get four thousand or so additional from a more worthy client."

He grinned indulgently and faced the girl. "Esther, what exactly did you run up against this morning?"

"Jensen's lawyer, for one thing. I never talked with a man who had so little to say and said it."

"And the National City. Was it friendly?"

"Cordial is a better word. They told me that everything was in the hands of a certain gentleman. To him I was conducted and introduced. He had nothing to offer, but plenty of questions to ask."

"I see. Was he a bank official?"

"Hardly. Not with his face and manner."

"I neglected to tell you," said Crole, rolling one of his flat cigarettes, "that L didn't want my name to appear."

"The neglect scarcely matters, Simon. I knew that if you wanted your name to appear, all you had to do was to call these people over your phone. The fact that you sent me made this obvious. I'm sorry I wasn't able to get anywheres with that man at the bank."

"Figure he was—a detective, for instance?"

"Plain clothes? Perhaps. But he wasn't a big man. Rather natty in a gray suit and . . ."

"Purple tie," finished Simon Crole.

Esther's eyes showed no surprise. "Lavender," she said.

Crole took out a handkerchief and mopped his bald head. "Purple," he insisted. "I had an interesting encounter with this same gentleman last evening, and came out second best."

14

LOOSE STRINGS

IT was mid-afternoon when Crole entered his office carrying the typewriter under his arm.

"Etta," he said to his secretary. "We've purchased a writing machine only recently abandoned by Mark Schilling. Mark had his reasons for getting rid of it. I planted a number of them in his mind. He believed me and got rid of the machine as if it were marked money."

"Does he know you have it?" asked Etta.

"Not yet. But he will sometime Monday. He'll offer me a handsome profit, but I don't know whether I'll sell it or not. You see, I'll demand something to boot—an original document. And without this original document there'll be no sale. In fact . . ."

The hall door opened. Captain Jorgens stepped through the opening. "In fact . . . what?" he asked.

"In fact," said Crole, pleasantly, grinning at the police officer, "I was just remarking to my secretary, Captain, that the person most interested in recovering the gun used on Officer Malloy would be you."

"Yeah? Well, where is said gun?"

"Softly, sir," said Crole. "I hadn't got around to actually giving you this information. I was holding it in reserve, as it were."

Captain Jorgens took a cigar from his pocket and clamped his teeth around it. From another pocket he took out a blueprint. "This," he said, "is the layout of the fifth floor of the Commerce building. The offices are all marked with the names of the lessees."

"Captain," said Crole, "we're getting somewheres. You want the gun. I want the blueprint. Swell. We'll exchange. But wait . . . I haven't got it. I had it. I'll swear to that, but it was lifted from my pocket by a man I thought was from the D. A.'s office. I've since decided that I guessed wrong on this guy."

"Don't be so damned long-winded. Tell me who the guy was and I'll pick him up."

"I don't know. I only . . ."

"Fat chance," muttered Jorgens, "of my giving you this blueprint. I should have known that there was some form of trickery . . ."

"You cops," said Crole, mildly, "are always quick on the trigger. You want to shoot first and talk afterwards, which isn't so hot, nor so pleasant. Give me a chance to explain."

"Hell, didn't you say that you didn't know who the guy was that took the gun away from you?"

"That's what I said, but what I didn't say was where the guy was to be found, and how he was dressed."

"Men can change clothes pretty easy."

"This guy won't be changing. He likes the suit and necktie he's wearing. And he'll keep on wearing them. Now you pay attention to me, Captain. And I'll see that you get your man. After that it's up to you to recover the gun."

He turned to his secretary. "Precious," he said. "Roll a sheet of paper into this machine I just brought in. Better make a carbon copy of what I'm going to dictate just in case . . ." He got to his feet and went over to the typewriter. "Put this down first; Written on L. C. Smith, serial number C-10290. Fine."

He sat down again. "Continue," he said. "The man who

took the gun from my pocket was of medium height, pointed face, wore a gray suit and purple tie. He is at present working with the officials of the National City Bank. How this gun came into my possession can be explained at the proper time—which isn't right now. Make a place for my signature, precious."

"You making that thing out for me?" asked Jorgens.

"Yeah. Figured you ought to have this thing down in writing. And a special kind of writing. Want to check the serial number on the machine?"

Captain Jorgens went over to the machine. "Sure. Why not."

"Mind okaying that part of what I have written?"

"Why should I?"

"What I dictated is written on a machine bearing a certain serial number. You saw my secretary write it. You compared the number on the machine with the number on this sheet of paper. They agree. All right. All I want is your initials after the number so that everything will come out all right in case anything happens to me."

"You figure," asked Jorgens, initialling both copies, "that maybe something will happen to you?"

"There's always a chance, Captain. I ain't ever held any lilies in my hand, but that doesn't mean I never will—not in my business. Maybe I'll fall out the window, or get socked over the head, or maybe I'll walk into some guy's gunfire."

Captain Jorgens took the cigar from between his teeth. He said unsmilingly: "I'd be the first to send a wreath, Simon." He examined his cigar for flaws. "You haven't, by any chance, turned up that black coupe, have you?"

"Not yet, but I expect to."

"Maybe you've got a fair idea right now where you can find it."

"Maybe I have." He shrugged. "As a matter of fact, Captain, the coupe is not as important as you might think."

"I prefer to place my own value on things, Simon."

"Of course. Don't blame you."

"I'll be going." With his hand on the hall door knob he turned back. "Getting back to your walking into somebody's gunfire. You wouldn't know who . . . ?"

"I wish I did," said Crole, wagging his head, sadly. "It's just one of those things I feel coming on. I can't explain it."

The Police captain looked as though he might say something more. Shrugged, and went out the door.

Simon Crole indicated the carbon copy with his index finger. "Put it in the safe, precious. Some day it's going to be valuable."

He went into his own office and spread the blueprint out on his desk. At the end of the hall was Schilling's office—apparently one large room. Next to it was an office labeled Atlas Contracting Company. On the other side of the hall was a dentist's suite of two rooms leased by a man named Painless Reilly. And adjoining the dentist's suite was a single room occupied by the Pacific Importing Company.

Crole studied their nearness one to the other. Next to the importing company was a washroom. That closed it from the rest of the offices. Across from it were the elevators.

It was possible, granting there were connecting doors, or wall panels as Matt had described, that one could go from any of these offices into Schilling's office at the end of the hall. It was also possible for anyone in the importer's office to watch the elevators.

Crole rolled a cigarette and lit it. Matt had followed O'Brien and had seen him enter the contractor's office. The panel that allowed him to walk into Schilling's room was evidently controlled by the fat man. But did the same thing exist, say from the suite of Painless Reilly? If so, it was just possible that police lieutenant Bemus occasionally paid the fat man a friendly visit.

But this was merely guessing. Maybe O'Brien didn't come through a panel from the contractor's office. Maybe it just appeared that way to Matt looking into the room at an angle.

Crole frowned, opened the desk drawer and placed the blueprint inside. He wondered what he had hoped to discover through its possession. His thoughts were like that. They came easily and were discarded quickly if they failed of their purpose. For several minutes he sat perfectly still, staring at nothing, his mind at work on a fresh line of action.

Presently he reached for the phone and called a number. "Esther," he said to his woman operator. "I want you to go to the apartment house where Charles Jensen lived. I imagine by now that the police have finished with their investigation and the landlord is looking for another tenant. Rent the apartment and everything that's in it. You needn't let on that you're aware of what happened in the apartment. You're a working girl and you need a place to eat and sleep."

Crole started to take the small memorandum book from his pocket, changed his mind, said: "Get the address from the telephone book. The apartment opens onto a court. Ground floor. And if the person in charge wants to clean the place, you say no! Tell whoever it is that you like to clean things yourself. Sure, I understand. There won't be much cleaning. Grab the apartment this afternoon, and pay a month's rent. See you tonight."

He hung up. Took the memorandum book from his pocket and made a few notations in a cipher known only to himself. It occurred to him, as he jotted down these notations, that he had a number of loose strings in his hands. The question in his mind was: which ones should he draw tight.

In the splendor of his office in the Commerce building, Mark Schilling was thinking much the same line of thought. In all things he was careful to watch and protect Mark Schilling. This was his creed—self-preservation by the surest and safest means.

This explains, partly, why he had surrounded himself with such an elaborate system of defense. He had certain men on his payroll who killed for a price. Willie Stevens, the sallow-faced man who sat in the importer's office and watched what took place in the hall, was of this breed. There were others who betrayed for a price. Vaguely, these men were aware of each other in the fat man's scheme of things. Actually, they knew little of each other.

Willie Stevens had seen Gat O'Brien come and go into Schilling's office via the Atlas Contracting Company. Willie knew him as the fat man's personal body-guard. But that was the extent of his knowledge. He was also aware of Lieutenant Bemus' many visits to Painless Reilly's office.

He did not know Reilly except by sight. He knew Bemus as a crooked cop. Beyond this slight knowledge he knew nothing, and cared even less, so long as the fat man paid him regularly.

Consequently, when Marie of the steel-trap mouth spoke crisply over the phone, he listened without special curiosity, abandoned his lookout position, and went at once to Schilling's office.

The pale eyes of the ponderous man in the chair were veiled. There was not the slightest trace of the fear and anger that was smouldering beneath the rolls of fat that covered his great body. His face was placid. He smoked his cigar with evident enjoyment.

But he was repeating over and over in his mind the creed by which he lived: Self-preservation by the surest and safest means.

"Willie," he said. "A careless man is potentially more dangerous to me than an outright betrayer. A betrayer makes only one mistake. That is enough. I know how to act regarding him. But a careless man makes many mistakes—honest ones, perhaps, yet these mistakes are a source of continual annoyance. But when a mistake turns into a serious blunder, dangerous for me and you as well, there is nothing for me to do but rid my organization of that man."

Willie Stevens nodded. "I getcha," he said. "Who's the guy."

The fat man wrote on a slip of paper. Willie looked at the writing. "Ahuh," he said. "When?"

"Tonight."

"Okay. Me and Dutch will handle it. And there won't be any kickback."

"Excellent," purred the fat man. "There will be five-hundred in it. The split will be three to two in your favor. I guess that's all, Willie."

Mark Schilling rubbed his jowls thoughtfully after his henchman had left. The fact that he had just sent a man to his death troubled his conscience not at all.

He took down the receiver and called a number not listed in the directory. "Has Mr. Yates," he said to the person who answered, "of the Chromium Novelty company attended to a very private matter? Fine. Pass the word along. Warn the boys to lay off any of the stores where his slot machines are set up."

He took the cigar from his mouth, placed it carefully on an ashtray and continued. "The Board held its meeting about the contract in the Filmore district. Did the Atlas people get their share? Not decided, eh? Well, put on pressure. You know where. And call me the first of the week if you see any signs of the Board getting cold feet. Bye."

He hung up and pressed a call button. The girl with the steel-trap mouth came in.

"Marie," he said. "There's an excellent opportunity of your making the equivalent of a month's salary at my place tonight. There's an old gentleman by the name of Fweeble, a client of Simon Crole's by the way, who is coming down to look the tables over. Be nice to him. And watch him. I don't know what Crole's game is. But I don't trust that private dick—nor Fweeble either, though Fweeble doesn't matter."

Marie said thinly: "I don't like the looks of that man Crole. He's got a queer smile—like as if he was laughing at you. I hate guys with faces like that. They do something to me inside. I want to dig my nails in their faces . . ."

"Control that temper of yours, Marie. If Crole gets in my way and becomes a nuisance . . ."

"More likely a menace," said Marie.

"If he becomes a menace, then," resumed the fat man, placidly, "I'll find a way to remove him from the picture. So don't antagonize the dick, and be especially nice to Fweeble. Suckers are scarce at the Casino these days. So play along with him. You'll draw funds for chips from the cashier."

Alone once more, he tapped lightly on the desk top with pudgy fingers. In much the same manner as Simon Crole, he stared into space at nothing at all, his pudgy fingers, mentally, touching the many threads of graft and corruption running through his hands. Some must be kept slack. Others must be tightened.

From his post of observation in the window of the building across the street from the Commerce structure, the patient Matt Ridley maintained a constant vigilance. He saw Willie Stevens appear, but he couldn't see Willie's features owing to the Venetian blinds that effectively covered the man's shoulders and face.

"A lousy set-up," he muttered, rubbing his neck grown stiff with the constant strain of facing the drawn curtain and peering through the two holes he had cut for his eyes. "I wish this window was about six feet farther up the street and lower down. I'm getting sick of this Peeping Tom job."

Not having seen Willie's face, he failed to recognize the man when he left the building a few minutes later. Still grumbling, Matt held his position at the window and was presently rewarded for his long-suffering patience.

Into his line of vision walked a man in the uniform of the police. How he got into the room Matt couldn't decide. But suddenly he was there.

Ridley's eyes bulged. "A cop!" he muttered, scratching his ear. And not from the traffic squad either. A headquarters man judging by what he could see of the trim uniform.

He started to leave his observation post. It was on his mind to get into immediate touch with Simon Crole. But he decided against it fearing the officer might leave the building while he was telephoning. And it was important that he see the officer's face.

The officer was striding up and down the room. Evidently he was more than a little excited. And as suddenly as he had appeared, he disappeared.

Matt Ridley, his eyes glued to the two holes cut in the window shade, waited for his quarry to reach the front sidewalk. He waited in vain. The man in the police uniform left the building through a rear door opening onto an alley which in turn led to the next street beyond, and Matt missed him entirely.

The phone rang after a long time. Matt took down the receiver. "Hello," he called.

"See anything of interest?" came Crole's voice over the wire.

Matt told him everything.

"Tough," said Crole. "But don't feel badly. You had the breaks once today. Can't expect them to keep up indefinitely. Better go out and get your supper. Then come back. I want you in a definite spot in case I need you later."

"Okay," agreed Matt. "I'll be right here till you call me off."

15

WITHIN THE CASINO

A TAXI with jeweled lights slid close to the curb and stopped before what had once been the dwelling place of an old Spanish grandee. It stood alone in isolated grandeur on a side street of the city that was trying so hard to be Metropolitan.

A seven-foot fence of metal spears enclosed it on four sides. It occupied half a city square. Surrounding it, like old, metal-clad retainers, were huge eucalyptus and pepper trees. There was a sunken garden on the south side, and the soft tinkle of water from a spraying fountain.

Only one thing marred its old-world setting—a concrete drive leading to a three-placed garage, the doors of which opened and closed mechanically, at the approach of a car. The outer gates through the metal spear fence had their regular attendants.

One of these looked sharply at the card August Fweeble extended. Without speaking he opened the gate. Three people walked through. It clanked behind them. The taxi with the jeweled lights pulled away from the curb.

The three people went up worn steps leading to an enormous, carved wooden door. The door was not, however, all wood. Behind it, reinforcing it, was a quarter inch sheet of nickel steel. As they went up the stairs a soft light from above the door played momentarily on their faces.

Again Fweeble showed his card. The door opened soundlessly into a reception room dimmed with shaded lights. An attendant took their wraps. A bowing manager in evening clothes was suddenly before them.

"Mr. Fweeble," he said. "I am glad to welcome you and your friends . . ."

Fweeble said: "Miss Manning, and Mr. Simon Crole."

The manager bowed to each in turn. "So glad to have you with us. You'll find refreshments in the Green Room off the lounge. The roulette tables are on the second floor."

Simon Crole's lips twisted into their smile of perpetual surprise. "A nice layout you've got here. I hope you won't mind if I clean the bank. I feel lucky tonight."

The manager's smile was perfection itself. "Occasionally that happens, Mr. Crole. Occasionally, but not often. The odds, of course, are against it unless you have the perfect system." He bowed again and moved off to welcome other patrons coming in the front entrance.

Esther took Simon Crole's arm as they went slowly up the thick-carpeted stairs. Her evening gown was of shimmering taffeta, cut daringly low in front, form-fitting, and flaring below the knees in delectable flounces. A scarlet cape of velvet, edged with white fox, and held together at the throat by a tiny golden chain, covered her shoulders.

"There's class to this place, Simon," she breathed into his ear. "Honestly, I feel positively pauperish with my little fifty dollars."

"Spread it out," said Crole. "Make it last." He turned to Fweeble. "What do you say, Gus. Think this place will suit you?"

The jaunty little man smiled oddly. "I'm sure it will if we have the right company. By the way, Mr. Crole," he added, as they stopped just outside the curtained doorway leading to the room where the roulette tables were placed. "I had a queer experience this afternoon."

Esther's fingers tightened their grip on her employer's arm.

Crole said: "Yeah? Get a ticket or something for speeding?"

"No," said Fweeble. "I met that police officer who was at our table at the Green Gate. The same man who came to your office . . ."

"You mean Captain Jorgens."

"The same. He was very much excited. There was a man with him who was in difficulty—a man with a gray suit. It seems that this man had a certain gun in his possession. I should judge that he was the same individual who took it from you at the curb in front of your office building the other night."

"So the police got him, huh?" Simon Crole's face was expressionless. "Maybe I'll get my gun back."

"I don't think so. The police seemed quite elated at having found it. It is my impression that they will keep it."

"Well," said Crole, "that would seem to be that."

"Let's go inside," said Esther. "We didn't come down here to talk about the police and guns."

"Excellent idea," agreed Fweeble.

Within the spacious room beyond the curtained doorway were three roulette tables. The hot glare of overhead lights illuminated two of the tables. Around them were gathered silent men and women with strained faces.

The *croupier* at the nearest table was calling mechanically: "Place your bets, gentlemen."

The trio edged closer. Esther found a vacant chair and slid into it. Simon Crole exchanged her fifty dollars for a like amount of chips. He bought two hundred dollars' worth for himself. When he next looked for Fweeble he found that individual had purchased at least three times that amount. Evidently the jaunty little man was preparing for a large evening.

They placed their bets along with the others. Crole decided to favor 11 and 19. From the end of the table there came a ratchet-like purring of the revolving wheel. A tiny silver ball raced within it. Gradually the wheel lost momentum. The silver ball began to waver. It dropped into a depression and popped out again. Then came to rest on number 23.

Crole heard Esther sigh with relief. She had two markers on 23. He covered 11 and 19 again. Lost. The *croupier's* voice droned on, endlessly it seemed.

Crole thought: "Two hundred dollars. I've got a feeling I'm gonna lose every nickel of it."

He bet on red. Black turned up. Red showed. He rubbed his bald head. Allowed three or four plays to pass, then switched in again to number 11 and won.

Grinning, he half-turned around to watch Esther and Fweeble. The girl's chips had doubled. While those of Fweeble were piled up like stacks of grain.

Crole sighed and switched to 23. When the silver ball came to rest, he blinked and shook his head. Bets were paid on number 19.

The crowd behind him pressed closer. Crole left the table and found a chair near the wall. He rolled a cigarette. Lit it, inhaled, and stared around him.

Presently he got to his feet and strolled casually to the second table. He didn't get in the game. Just stood there and studied faces. After a time he left and went out into the hall.

The suave manager was suddenly before him, bowing from the hips. "Are you engaged right now?" he asked.

Crole wagged his head slowly. "No," he said. "The pace was too swift. Thought I'd walk around and see if my luck would change."

The manager nodded. "Will you follow me, Mr. Crole? There's a gentleman that would like a few words with you."

"And the gentleman's name?" asked Crole.

"Mr. Schilling."

"Fine. I was hoping that I would see him."

The manager turned without another word and led the private detective through velvet hangings into a narrow hall at the end of which was a door labeled 'Private'.

He knocked twice, opened it and bowed Crole in. The detective entered. The door closed with a slight click. Crole's first impression of the room was an enormous safe. From the safe his eyes wandered to the fat man sitting in a chair behind a desk.

Schilling said through lips that barely moved. "What's the idea, Crole, of you coming here to my place?"

Simon Crole didn't immediately answer. He dropped into a chair, took out his tobacco sack and rolled a flat-cigarette. "The idea, Schilling," he said, squinting along the gummed edge of the cigarette, "was to win some of your money. Business is slack you know. What with the loss of clients and other such unfortunate reverses. But your number-one table cleaned me of a hundred and fifty bucks before I knew what was happening."

"You aren't by any chance going to register a complaint?"

"Who, me? Complain? No, nothing like that. But losing money always makes me sad, Schilling. I'm funny that way."

"You're going to lose more money, Crole."

Crole's bald head cocked sideways. "So?"

Schilling's fat chins quivered. "Yes, you're going to take a big loss on your former client, Judge Chadwick."

"That's news to me, Schilling. If I remember right I was to call at your office on Monday . . ."

"It won't be necessary. We'll conclude our business this evening. Here. There's no reason I can see for letting it ride."

Simon Crole blinked pleasantly. "Your vision, Schilling, is slightly warped. You see one thing. I see another."

"Judge Chadwick," resumed the fat man, smiling coldly, "refuses to have anything more to do with the matter. I think that lets you out, Crole. I'm sorry . . ."

"So am I. I really am, Schilling. It means that I'll have to turn that photostat copy of Nicky Lombardo's statement over to the police. And that will bring me a lot of notoriety and bother from the dicks at headquarters."

"That's your hard luck."

"I guess it is, Schilling. That's the way it looks. And I don't like to do it. It means I've got to scramble around and protect myself. If Captain Jorgens should ever find that machine in my office . . ."

"Machine!" Schilling's voice was slightly higher in pitch. "What machine are you talking about?"

"I forgot to tell you, Schilling, but it's a fact. I've got the typewriter used in making the original statement. Ain't that the berries? And I wouldn't want Captain Jorgens to know I've got it. Embarrassing you know. Lots of explanations. Hard to explain to police. They're so headstrong." He sighed and leaned back in the chair.

"You're sure you've got *the* machine, Crole?"

"Oh, yes. I've got it all right. Picked it up in a secondhand store. Funny thing how it happened. A guy just brought it in. The dealer didn't have it on his shelf more'n a couple minutes. You remember me telling you about the peculiar oddities of the type. Horizontal line of the 'e' broken. Capital 'N' sort of haywire. An expert would trace the whole alphabet and . . ."

"Pretty smart dick," observed Schilling, tapping the desk top with pudgy fingers. "You wouldn't know by any chance the name of the man who sold the machine to the second-hand dealer?"

Crole shook his head. "No," he lied. "I wouldn't know that. But I do know I've got the machine." He crushed his cigarette in an ashtray. "I guess we've finished, Schilling. Got to get back to the tables. My friends will be wondering what happened to me."

"Your friends," drawled the fat man, "have not missed you."

He leaned forward in his chair. His pale eyes seemed to retreat into the back of his skull. "Your having this machine sort of complicates things, Crole."

"It will complicate things for the police, but not for me. I'm getting out. Running too close to legality makes me worry. Withholding information . . ."

"Is a serious offense," finished Schilling. "I realize that as well as you do, Crole."

The private detective said nothing.

The fat man resumed. "The risk, however, may be worth your while, provided . . ."

"Provided," said Crole.

"Provided I can explain things satisfactorily to Judge Chadwick."

"I fail to see why the judge has anything to say about it. You told me he wasn't interested and refused to have anything to do with the matter. That cleans me up. Why should I hang on to a hot piece of evidence like this typewriter and place my own reputation in jeopardy?"

"Your reputation is not spotless, Crole."

"Perhaps not. But it happens to be my reputation."

"And you still insist upon turning this machine over to the police?"

"What else can I do?"

"I wonder," said Schilling, pursing his lips. "The judge is away for the week-end. He won't be back until Monday. If you could wait until then, I can promise to place your grievance squarely before him and I'm positive he'll pay you for the machine this time. Forty-five hundred wasn't it?"

Crole nodded. "That's right. But I still don't see why he should want it. It looks funny on the surface."

"On the surface perhaps it does. But Judge Chadwick is a thorough man. He believes in getting at the bottom of everything. He may decide to conduct the investigation himself by tracing the man who sold the machine to the second-hand dealer."

"I'll give him," said Crole, getting to his feet, "till Monday night. If I don't hear favorably from you by then, all bets are off."

"You're acting wisely, as I knew you would," said the fat

man. "Have a cigar before you go?"

Crole shook his head. "No thanks. I'm strong for a rolled cigarette. Anything else tastes like alfalfa." He grinned pleasantly and returned to the roulette room.

"I'm lousy rich," thrilled Esther. "Nearly a thousand . . ."

"Where's Gus?"

"Number 2 table. He's got himself a companion. Name is Marie. Someone introduced them. They're great friends already."

"Wait here," said Crole. "Don't sit in on any more games. I've got a feeling we're pulling out, pronto." He left the girl operator at the fringe of table one and strolled over to the second table.

The click of markers and the hum of the wheel was the only sound heard in the big room. Then as the silver ball settled into place there came one or two happy sighs, a rustle of feet, and then the white-faced *croupier's* mechanical song: "Place your bets, gentlemen."

He found Fweeble wedged between a dowager heavily draped with pearls, and a sprightly young thing who was vaguely familiar. At the sound of his voice Fweeble turned around. His face was calm and inscrutable. Before him was a huge stack of chips.

"Hello, Mr. Crole," he said. "Meet my friend, Marie."

The girl turned around. Crole recognized her at once. He smiled. "We've met before," he said. "How are you?"

The steel-trap mouth smiled thinly. "Just fine, thanks."

"Don't thank me," said Crole. "Gus," he said to his jaunty little man. "I gotta leave. Miss Manning is ready to quit now that she's ahead. I am, too, but not for the same reason. I almost lost my shirt. Besides we want to take in a show. See you some other time, huh?"

"Well, well," spluttered Fweeble. "Er, can't this be arranged somehow. Perhaps I've neglected my duties as a host . . ."

"Forget it," said Crole. "Have a good time, Gus. Sorry we've got to run along, but I just gotta see that show."

Fweeble blinked rapidly. "Yes, yes, of course. Well, er . . . to be sure you've got to see the show. I hope . . . I trust, Mr. Crole, that my asking you to accompany me here this evening hasn't inconvenienced you . . . er, financially."

"Nothing like that, Gus. I just got fed up and decided I wanted to take in a show. G'night." He waved airily, swung around and started towards the spot where he had left Esther.

He looked back once over his shoulder. Fweeble and Marie were bent over the dull green felt of the table, fingering their markers as they waited for the next turn of the wheel.

"Come, Esther," he said to the girl. "We're off to a show."

"A show?" There was neither surprise nor anxiety in the girl's face. "What show? Where?"

"You'd be surprised if I told you. Something I arranged on the spur of the moment. If I'm not mistaken in my man, the office of Simon Crole, special investigator, will be entered illegally sometime during the night and a hot piece of evidence will be taken therefrom."

Esther pawed in her handbag which contained among other things, a .25 caliber Spanish-make automatic. She took from the bag a small mirror and held it before her face.

"I hope," she said, quietly, "as I've heard you remark to police Captain Jorgens, that you know what you're doing."

Simon Crole's shoulders lifted in a barely perceptible shrug. "I know exactly what I'm doing. It's what the other fellow is going to do that keeps me awake nights."

16

NIGHT MOVES ON

THE suave manager was bowing politely before them as they waited for the attendant to bring their wraps.

"I trust," he said, "that you've had a pleasant, if not a profitable evening, Mr. Crole."

"The evening," Crole said, drily, "was not what one might by any stretch of the imagination be called profitable. I think I'd prefer to finish it at a theatre. Gambling bores me—when I lose."

"I find most of our friends and visitors are afflicted the same way. All of us can't win, of course." He bowed again and drifted silently away.

On their way through the door leading to the outer steps they passed two men who were just arriving. Their jaws, Crole noticed, paying attention as always to the unusual, were set in rigid lines. Their eyes stared neither right or left, but straight ahead. One of them had a bruise on his left cheek.

"Willie Stevens," thought Crole, remembering back to a time when Captain Jorgens had pointed him out in the morning line-up. He recalled also Gordon Chadwick's mentioning a man named 'Willie' of whom he had heard Lombardo speak. This must be the man. But what was he doing here in this exclusive gambling house?

Stevens, he recalled, was not a big shot. He was out of his element here among the swells. Very much out of his element. The private detective wished he hadn't left quite so abruptly as he did. He would have liked to have followed Stevens and his companion up the stairs. However, he realized that this was impossible. But nothing could prevent having the two men followed when they returned again to the street. This, he decided to do.

Esther's fingers were gripping his arm. "Those two men," she said. "Who were they?"

"Couple of Mark's muscle men, I think," observed Crole once they had reached the sidewalk and had passed through the iron gates.

"I saw the one with the yellowish face leave the Commerce building once," said the girl.

"That checks," said Crole. "Good girl. I know what to do, now."

He waved a taxi to the curb and helped her inside. After they were settled and the machine had started he took one of her hands between his own. "How's your nerve?" he asked.

Esther smiled brightly. Feminine to her finger tips, there was no trace visible of the endurance, strength and fearlessness in the soft curves of her splendid young body. "Nerves are okay, Simon," she said. "I could do with a drink. You forgot to get me a cocktail back there in the Casino, for which I'll never forgive you."

"I was negligent," said Crole. "Forgive me. We get out here."

The machine stopped barely two blocks away from the Casino. Crole paid the driver, took the girl by the arm, and started up town. As soon as the taxi had rounded a corner, he guided her back down the street from whence they had come.

A block from the Casino he stopped. "Those two hoods," he said. "They'll be coming out soon. Tail them. I'm sending a cab down to pick you up. The driver will be someone you can trust."

"You think these men will go to your office . . ."

"I don't know. That's why I'm having you follow them when they leave the Casino. Now give me the key to Jensen's old apartment. Seems as though all I do is rent places. I'm getting old, dear, when I can't handle a case from my own office."

Esther said: "Why did you have me rent that apartment?"

"I've asked myself that question several times. I don't know exactly. But I've got a hunch that there's considerable money in that place. I don't think the man who hung Jensen got it. Nor Schilling either."

"Then who . . ."

"I still don't know. The police searched the place, and I imagine they did a thorough job. Turned it completely upside down. Not even the keys to safety deposit boxes were uncovered. Now I'm to take up where they left off. Maybe I won't have any more luck than the police."

He looked carefully around the darkened street and continued: "Now don't take any chances with these hoods. Stay in the cab I send down to pick you up. All I expect of you is a report on any buildings they enter. Remember, Matt is in the new office. You know the number. If you get into a jam, or what looks like the beginning of one, give him a ring." He squeezed her hand again, pivoted and went up the street.

At a drugstore he called a number. "Chief dispatcher? This is Simon Crole. Is George Scavillo's cab in the rank? Good. Tell him who's hiring it, and have him drive to the corner one block north from the Casino. He'll know where it is. There, he's to pick up one of my operators, a young woman. But don't send anyone but Scavillo. Okay." He hung up, waited a minute then called another number.

"Hello, Matt," he said. "Any activity across the street? Thought not. Just left the fat man in his private office at the Casino. But how long he'll be there I don't know. Stick to your post. I may need you later. No, I won't be at the office. I'm going someplace else."

He paused for emphasis. "Listen some more. Esther is in Scavillo's cab tailing a couple of Schilling's hoods. I think she'll be safe enough if she doesn't leave the cab. I told her not to. But be ready in case anything breaks. Bye." He hung up.

On the street outside Crole rolled a cigarette and lit it. The hands of a clock in a jewelry store pointed to eleven. He walked up the street till he found a cab. He got in and was driven through the night streets to within a block of Jensen's old apartment.

Making certain he hadn't been followed, he kept in the shadows till he reached an alley, turned in, found himself in the court. There were very few lights showing in the building. He let himself in, closed and locked the door behind him. Drew down the shades and switched on all the lights.

The rooms had been straightened and cleaned. Feminine apparel was strewn about the bedroom. There were crackers, cheese, lime-ricky bottles and a quart of gin in and nearby the electric refrigerator.

Crole mixed a cocktail, and sipping it leisurely went back to the living room. Once again he sat in the deep chair and mentally reviewed everything that had taken place from the moment he had seen the pair of men's shoes hanging in the air, till his abrupt departure.

As memory rebuilt the gruesome scene he could see the body of the crooked cashier swaying lightly at the end of the rope. The victim's mouth was closed, lips drawn in. The Medical Examiner had remarked on this, stating that it looked as if the strangling man was attempting to say something when speech was cut off.

If that was the case, Jensen was being tortured to make him reveal the hiding place of the money. But the fact that the apartment had been ransacked afterwards, proved that the murderer had not been successful in making Jensen reveal the hiding place.

What had happened, then? The rope was around Jensen's

neck. He was standing on the beer-bottle case. Then something happened. Something frightened the killer. A telephone ring, or a knock at the door. He drew away from his victim, undecided, fearful of interruption. Perhaps he went over to the door.

While he was crouching beside the door something happened to Jensen. Perhaps he fainted. Or became suddenly frantic. His feet somehow . . . No! That wasn't the answer. The marks on the beam proved conclusively that the body had been dragged upward.

Crole's forehead puckered with concentration wrinkles. He was thinking of those indrawn lips. Jensen had died quickly. The word that was forming on his lips had never been uttered. The clue was there, but it eluded him.

He went out into the kitchen again and mixed himself a second cocktail. As he slowly sipped it he was aware once more of the Medical Examiner standing on the table making ready to cut the body down. The cops were below waiting for it to drop into their arms.

Crole saw again the flash of the knife blade. Saw the rope strands snap apart. Then his ears were profaned again by the eerie howl coming from the mouth of the corpse.

'Fi . . . eeee . . . ooow!' Something cold slithered down the detective's spine. He finished his drink and set the glass down.

The wrinkles in his forehead began to smooth out. The answer was not far away. He was beginning to perceive it dimly. The clue was in the sound forced from the mouth of the corpse —a partly formed word, and a succession of vowels. The key was in the first word consisting of a consonant and a short vowel.

Simon Crole endeavored to complete the unfinished word. "Fit," he began. "Finish . . . finicky . . . Finnegan . . . fifth . . . fin . . . fish . . . !" He stopped and repeated the last word. The fanwise wrinkles radiating outwards from his eyes deepened with concentration.

He recalled without conscious effort the report of the Austrian chemist. Other things had crowded it from his mind. "Silicon," he mumbled, "quartz particles, dried fronds, commercial lacquer . . ."

The pieces dropped suddenly in their proper place, and the picture was beautifully complete. He slapped his thighs, grinned, and went slowly across the room towards the one object in the room that everyone had overlooked.

The pale eyes of the fat man turned slowly from the face of Willie Stevens to that of the second man, Dutch Peters. What he saw pleased him. He said nothing for the moment.

"We got him," said Willie, clearing his throat. "He's croaked."

"Where?"

"Rooming house, west 19th."

"Gunplay?"

"Naw. Lead pipe. We doped his drink. He was half asleep. I brought the pipe down on his head. Twice. Something inside cracked. He fell off the chair he was sitting in, and curled up in a heap."

"The glasses," said the fat man, thinking fast.

"Don't worry," said Dutch Peters. "They was half a dozen or so on the table along with the bottles. I wiped 'em dry on a towel. No prints left. We was careful all right."

"Anybody see you come or go?"

"It was dark. We slipped in quietly. Came out the same way."

Schilling took five century notes from a desk drawer and handed them to Willie. "Satisfied?"

Willie handed two of them to Peters. He said nothing.

The fat man moistened his lips with a probing tongue. He said: "When men cease to be useful to me, they go—by the short way. As long as that man lived, our organization was in danger."

Peters said: "*You* were in danger—not us." His ugly face twisted for a moment as if his thoughts were unpleasant things. "How about Larkin, while we're on the subject? He wasn't a bad guy. Didn't squawk or nothing. Whyn't the organization help him? We're losing guys fast. Nicky, then Strangler, and now . . ."

"You, guy," cut in Willie, thinly, "keep your trap shut. You got two century notes for wiping a couple glasses. Me, I did the croaking. Either you're satisfied or you ain't."

"I'm satisfied, but just the same—hell, can't a guy wonder?"

Willie stared at his companion. In his slow-working brain an ugly thought took root. He wasn't aware of it at once. It came over his mind by slow degrees. Maybe, when Schilling had finished with him, he'd go the same way as the others.

But Schilling wouldn't do this to him. He was the fat man's number one strong-arm guy. He was safe. Peters was getting scared. Schilling was all right. Sure he was. Willie took a handkerchief from his pocket and wiped the bruise on his cheek.

"Dutch is jumpy, Chief, I can handle him. Guess we'd better blow now, hey?"

Mark Schilling's head moved ponderously on his thick neck. "Not yet. I've got another job for you and Dutch. But of a different kind. Evidence plant. Same pay. It will have to be handled tonight. If you don't want it, say so. And I'll get someone else."

Willie said: "We'll take it."

"All right," said the fat man. "Now listen, and listen carefully. I don't want any mistakes . . ." He paused significantly, "like the last man made."

"There won't be no mistakes," said Willie Stevens. "I ain't made any yet, have I?"

A facial twisting intended for a smile passed over the fat man's face. "No, Willie, you haven't made any mistakes—yet."

Willie Stevens stared dully into the inscrutable eyes of Mark Schilling. He didn't like the way the fat man had uttered the word 'yet', and he couldn't quite understand the pause before it was uttered.

Marie came suddenly through the door behind him. He twisted slowly and moved away from the desk.

"Well, Marie?" said Schilling, pleasantly.

"Say, listen," said the girl with the steel-trap mouth. "What did you send me up against. That guy was no sucker. He knows more about roulette than the guy that invented the game. He cleaned up plenty and never passed me over a single chip."

Schilling rubbed his chins thoughtfully. "Get Barney to open the number 3 table."

"Swell chance. The old guy beat it. Walked out on me just like I was a chair or something. Said he was going downstairs to get me a drink. And like a sap I believed him. He never came back."

"You should have gone with him."

"You telling me? How was I to know what kind of a mugg

he was? There I was sitting in a chair. I had everything fixed
with him. He was taking me down to the World Exposition at
San Diego so he said. And all the time he was cleaning up and
salting it away in his pocket."

"Unfortunate," drawled the fat man. "But you must have
made him cagey. Come back later. I'm busy with the boys right
now."

"Oh, I'll be back all right," snarled the girl, leaving the room
and slamming the door behind her.

"Nice kid," observed Willie. "I'd show her a good time myself, if she'd let me."

"You leave her alone," said the fat man, ominously. "She
has her uses in my scheme of things. And they don't include a
punk like *you*."

The face of Willie Stevens twisted into something intended
for a smile—but it was more like the grin of a frozen fish. The
seed of ugly suspicion against the fat man, planted in his mind
by Dutch Peters, was slowly beginning to sprout weeds of hate.

His mind reverted to Larkin now in the big house; of
Strangler with a rope hung around his neck in the waters of the
estuary; of the man he had slugged that night. And like Dutch
Peters, he, too, began to wonder.

Some of these days, he knew, his own time would come. He
would do something that the fat man wouldn't like. Curtains for
Willie. It struck him pleasantly, since he was a cold-blooded
killer, that he would get a hell of a lot of satisfaction in drawing
a knife across those many chins of the fat man, just to see what
would happen.

He was still grinning like a frozen fish when he said: "Okay,
Chief, I was only kidding about the skirt."

Mark Schilling bit the end off a cigar, spat it out, and said:
"Well, boys, it's like this . . ."

The woman with the dyed hair almost snarled at Captain
Jorgens. "How should I know," she said. "I called you, didn't
I, on the telephone. I said they was a dead man in one of my
rooms. And that's all I know."

Jorgens eyed her queerly. "How come you went in his
room?"

"He owed me a week's rent. Due on Saturday, today. I went

in to get it. Sometimes he leaves it on the dresser. He always was good about paying me Saturday. And this is the way I found him. I run to the telephone quick as I could."

The police captain swore softly. "All right," he said. "Get out. I'll call you when I'm ready to talk with you again. Sergeant, keep your eye on her. Don't let her out of the building."

The Medical Examiner came in humming the latest dance number. "H'are you, Captain? Another victim bit the dust, eh? Tsk, tsk. What a terrible world this is getting to be."

"Aren't you ever serious, Doc?" grouched the police captain.

The Medical Examiner moved about briskly. "Serious? In *my* work? I'd go nerts in a couple months if I took life as hard as you do, Captain. Yes sir, I'd go completely nerts."

He bent over the silent figure on the floor. "Ummmm! Temporal bone crushed in. Cerebral hemorrhage. Eyes wide and staring. Didn't bleed much. Clotted inside." His skillful fingers parted the matted hair. "Something hard and heavy. Lead pipe probably." He rolled the body over.

"Hey," he said. "He's got a glass in his fingers. Must have had it there when struck down. Now that's nice, maybe."

Captain Jorgens took the glass from the stiffened fingers with a folded handkerchief. He handed it to the fingerprint expert who was dusting powder on the bottles and glasses found on the table.

"Ah!" said the expert. "It's about time. Them bottles and glasses are as clean as if scrubbed by a barkeep. But this one's got plenty of marks on it."

Jorgens called in two of his men from the hall. "Look around, boys, for a chunk of pipe. The windows were open. You might find it in the back lot." He knelt beside the Medical Examiner.

"Find anything else, Doc?"

"Nope. Not a thing. Been dead about two hours and a half. Better have the stuff in that glass examined. Eyes look funny. He was doped I think. Murder all right, Captain. He didn't die from the dope, however. He died from that crack on the head. A wicked smash. Wait a second. Two of them. He was struck twice almost in the same place."

Jorgens said dourly: "As if one blow wasn't enough." He raised his eyes. There was a commotion in the hall. In the doorway stood Simon Crole.

17

ESTHER IN A JAM

POLICE CAPTAIN JORGENS' lidded eyes stared hard on the agency man in the doorway. "Thought it was about time you showed up. Why didn't you get here before? Why wasn't it you that called me instead of that old hag with the dyed hair? Why . . . ?"

"Why the tirade?" asked Crole, blandly. "I ain't to blame for everything that goes on. I go down to your office to chew the rag with you, and I get there right after you left. So I tags along, and here I am."

"Here you am!" snapped Jorgens, crossly. "Get the hell out of my sight. I'm tired of looking at that mug of yours."

"Get tired of looking at it myself, Captain—at times. Evening, Doc," he grinned on the Medical Examiner, "or is it morning. *Tempus fugit,* as the Greeks used to say."

"Romans," corrected the Medical Examiner, yawning. "Well, Captain, it looks like you got another murder on your hands. That's the way I'm writing the ticket. Will somebody pass me a cigarette?"

No one had cigarettes, so none were passed.

"I suppose," said Jorgens, his voice soaked with sarcasm, "that you know all about this corpse, Simon; who he was, his age, friends, habits, reason for being bumped off . . ."

"You suppose all wrong," said Crole, taking out his tobacco sack and rolling a cigarette. He was aware of the Medical Examiner making overt gestures. He pretended not to see for the sack was nearly empty.

"Thank God for that," sighed the police officer.

Crole bent and took a look at the dead man's face. "Gat O'Brien," he said. "Too bad. A man makes a mistake, then he's rubbed out. Dead men don't make second mistakes. The way this mob is being rubbed out . . ."

"What mob?" Jorgens chewed belligerently on his black cigar.

"Just a few of the boys," said Crole, inhaling deeply. "Larkin, Nicky Lombardo, and Gat O'Brien all worked for the same boss. They make mistakes, and then everything's off between them and their boss."

Jorgens tried to sneak in a simple question. "What boss?"

"I wouldn't know," said Crole, wagging his head. "I wish I did, Captain. Stands to reason they must have had a boss, doesn't it?"

Lieutenant Bemus entered. He shouldered Crole one side and went up to his superior. "What's this private dick doing here, Captain. You know the Chief don't like guys like him hanging around. Who's been bumped off this time?"

Captain Jorgens took the cigar from between his teeth. "A mobster, name of O'Brien."

"The hell!" gasped Bemus. "Not Gat O'Brien?"

"You know him?"

Bemus backed water. "Why, yes, slightly. I've seen him around."

"Around who?"

"Around town. One of our stools pointed him out once."

"Maybe you can find out from that stool who he hung around with. It's important. Get busy on that angle. There's nothing more to be done here."

"I'll see what I can do," said Bemus, hurrying from the room.

Crole said casually: "Bemus ever have any trouble with his teeth, Captain?"

"Who, him? No. His last medical examination showed them perfect." He frowned. "You ask the damnedest questions. What's in the back of that bald head of yours?"

"I wonder myself sometimes. Must have a nasty mind. How much longer will you be on duty?"

"I go off at six. Or I'm supposed to."

"Maybe you'll hear from me by then. Meantime, when next you see Bemus, ask him what he thinks professionally of Painless Reilly."

"Who the devil is Painless Reilly?"

"A dentist with offices in the Commerce Building."

The police captain gripped the arm of Crole and guided him to a far corner of the room where their voices wouldn't be heard by the others. "Listen, Simon," he said, hoarsely. "This can't go on indefinitely. We've got to have a clear understanding of how we stand in this business. The D. A. is riding me hard. So are the newshawks. Ever since you phoned Farrel, his paper has been filled with ugly insinuations."

Crole blinked rapidly. "Stall along, Captain," he advised. "I may have a hot lead for you within a couple hours. But I can't tip off my hand until I'm ready."

"Then you know!" Jorgen's eyes glittered hopefully. "It's you that's doing the stalling."

"I'm guessing, Captain. Leave me alone. I've got to handle things in my own way. I don't know anything about the bumping-off of this guy O'Brien. But I can guess. What I wanted to see you about was this: You recall that typed specimen of the work done on the machine in my office?"

Jorgens nodded.

"Do any of your subordinates know about it?"

"No. I've still got it in my pocket."

"Keep it there. Keep this, too." He handed the police officer a parcel check. "If anything happens to me, you're to get this package. But you're not to get it unless something happens to me. I want it clearly understood that way."

Jorgens pocketed the check stub. "That all?"

Crole nodded. "That's all. See you later. G'bye."

He went out of the rooming house and took a cab to the building where he had his office. There were one or two private cars parked at the curb, and one taxi. Crole examined it in passing. It was not the cab of George Scavillo. He walked down the block on both sides of the street in hopes of finding Esther. She was not visible anywheres.

He glanced up at his office windows. No light showed. He went in. The elevator cages were darkened. Crole sighed and puffed up seven flights of stairs. Inserted the key to the hall door. Swung the door inward and snapped on the lights.

He closed the door behind him and stood rocking on his heels. A wry smile crossed his face. So far as he could see, nothing had been disturbed. The typewriter was still on the desk where his secretary had last used it.

Crole crossed to it and idly tapped its keys. Schilling hadn't taken the bait this time. Why? Was he afraid? Or had he something else in mind?

He sat down at his secretary's desk. Across the darkened building tops outside came a dolorous chime. One o'clock. He took the receiver from its hook and spoke a number into the mouthpiece.

Matt Ridley answered at once, his voice breaking with excitement. "Boss, I've been trying to locate you for the last ten minutes. Scavillo called up. Esther gave him my number when she left his cab half an hour after midnight. She hasn't come back yet. I was going down to investigate, but I didn't want to leave . . ."

Crole said: "Where did she leave the cab?"

"Five hundred block, Eighty-seventh street. Scavillo's there now, still waiting."

"I'm going after her." He swore softly. "I never should have sent her . . . You stay where you are, Matt. I'll get in touch with you if I need you."

"Better let me go with you. I'm scared as hell that the kid's in a jam with them hoods she was tailing."

"I'm scared, too," admitted Crole.

He hung up and lurched to his feet. He didn't look scared. His jaw was slightly outthrust. His gray eyes were almost closed. His step was firm as he crossed the floor to his inner office. He opened a desk drawer containing a private arsenal.

There were three ugly-snouted automatics in the drawer. He looked at them longingly, shook his head, and reached behind them for a different kind of a weapon.

The blackjack was a marvel of the saddler's art. The leather was stretched tautly over leaden shot and served with cunning stitches. A braided thong enabled the user to hold it snugly to the wrist. Crole hefted it carefully, made certain that the looped thong would slide easily onto his wrist, pocketed it, snapped out the lights and went down the seven flights of stairs to the street.

He found Scavillo's cab drawn close to the curb at the corner of 87th street. He opened the door and climbed in. "Where's my operator, Scavillo?"

"Geez, Mr. Crole," breathed the cab driver. "I'm glad you're here. I was worried to beat hell."

"Get on with the story," snapped the agency man.

"Sure," said the cabman. "I picked her up like you ordered. We tailed two guys in another cab downtown near your office.

Your op got out and followed the two guys in the other machine. After a time they come back. And so does your op."

He paused. "Well, we followed 'em through the city. It looked like they was wise to the fact that we was tailing 'em. I'd let other cars get between us, but I never lost sight of the machine once. The cab finally stopped on this street. Six houses from the corner. Your op got out and walked down that way slowly. She didn't come back. I got nervous and called the number she gave me."

"Sixth house from the corner," said Crole, grimly. "You wait here, Scavillo. If I'm not back in half an hour, call Captain Jorgens at police headquarters. But I'll be back."

Thrusting his right hand deep in his coat pocket, he walked slowly down the darkened street. He came abreast of the sixth house. It was dark. Not a light was visible in any of its windows.

Simon Crole went up the walk. Climbed two steps to the porch and punched the electric bell. He heard it sound deep within the building. He waited a moment then punched it again.

The door opened suddenly. A beam of light splashed from the black interior into the detective's face.

"What do you want?"

"I want in," Crole said, thrusting his shoulder against the door.

"Out!" snarled the voice.

Crole's arm traveled up and down. The man squawked and slumped across the door sill. The agency man stepped over his body. He fumbled for the light switch, found it, and turned it on. He continued on through a hall towards the sound of voices.

A knob twisted beneath his fingers. He flung the door wide. The room was empty except for the roped figure of a woman on a davenport. The sound of voices came from a radio. Crole snapped it off and went over to the davenport.

Esther's mouth was bandaged. She must have put up considerable fight for the shimmering taffeta dress was almost torn from the upper part of her body. There were marks dull red in color on her shoulders, and a darkish bruise on her left cheek. Her eyes were bright as they looked up at him.

He took the gag from her mouth. "Don't talk," he said, "till we get outside." He cut the rope binding her ankles and wrists, helped her to a standing position, and picked up the red velvet cape tossed in a corner. He placed it around her bare shoulders.

She swayed slightly. "Dizzy," she said, collapsing to the davenport. "Be all right in a second."

The detective picked her up bodily and carried her through the hall to the front door. He glanced down at the man blocking the doorway. Saw that his eyes were open and charged with venom.

He kicked the gun from the man's fingers and stood the girl on her feet outside so that she could lean against the door sill.

"Did this guy get fresh with you?" His voice was metallic. He noticed again the bruises on her cheek.

"He got rough when I wouldn't talk."

Simon Crole swallowed heavily. "The cab is down at the corner. Can you make it?"

"Yes, I think so."

"Get going. Don't stop for anything."

The man on the floor was struggling to his feet. He had a knife in his hand. He swung with it just as Crole turned from helping Esther down the two steps to the walk.

Crole hit him. Hit him with bunched knuckles. His hand travelled less than six inches. The man fell like a poled ox. Crole dragged him erect by the collar and hit him again.

The man's eyes were glassy. Crole grunted and relinquished his grip. His anger cooled. He knelt beside the man on the floor. "You want more of the same brand?" he asked.

"No," gasped the man. "Quit it."

"Ready to talk?"

"Nothing to say."

"Where are those two hoods that came in here."

"Try and find out."

"My knuckles feel swell," Crole said, lifting the man to a sitting position. "This isn't gonna hurt till you wake up."

"Them gorillas will rub you out . . ."

"Shut up! I've been treating you gentle. Now I'm gonna get rough. Get up. You're going for a ride."

"No!"

Crole sighed and jerked the man to his feet. "We'll see."

The man kicked the detective in the shins. As the agency

man instinctively lurched forward the man jammed an elbow
into Crole's neck. This was the last straw. Gasping for breath
he brought the leather-bound blackjack down hard. Thock!

The desk sergeant looked down on the trio before his desk.
"What the big idea?" he asked.

"Lock this guy up," blustered Crole, "before I get mad and
kill him. He got rough with a friend of mine, a lady friend."

"He's a liar," snarled the prisoner. "He busted into my house.
He hit me with a blackjack. He . . ."

Captain Jorgens strolled out of his private office. He looked
from Esther to Crole to the prisoner. Crole's eyes showed no
signs of recognition.

"You the big noise in this dump?" he asked.

"What is this," asked Jorgens. "A brawl?"

"Brawl nothing," protested the agency man. "This guy here
grabs my lady-friend—makes a snatch . . ."

"Shut up!" interrupted the police officer. "So, it's Hardboiled
Connely, eh? Where the hell you been lying up? Maybe you
think that because you're no longer in the big house that you
don't have to check in once in a while."

Connely glared viciously. "The big guy's a liar. He hit me
with a sap. He broke into my house . . ."

"Look at my girl friend," said Crole. "He marked her up
plenty—he and two other guys." His gray eyes flung warning
signals in the captain's direction. And his chin moved slightly
up. "Those two other guys bumped off a friend of mine," he
hurried on. "I heard all about how they done it through a fat
guy that runs a swell gambling joint. This fat guy tips me off . . ."

"Hey," yelled Connely, "Button up your lip."

"It's my lip," growled the agency man, "and I won't button
it up. Did I know who they was I'd bump 'em off myself.
Why'd they give Gat the works?" He shook his knotted fist beneath Connely's swollen jaw. "Gat was no enemy of theirs. I
know that for a fact."

"Hey, mugg," snapped Jorgens, his powerful fingers on
Crole's shoulder. "You got altogether too much to say around
here."

"Gat was my friend," insisted the agency man, driving hard
on the idea. "And he was killed by two hoods, friends of this

guy, Hardboiled Connely. A fat man told me—a fat man who's a big shot in this city. I know what I'm talking about. I know . . ."

"You're drunk," growled Jorgens. "Take your woman and get out. No. Wait!" He turned to Hardboiled Connely. "You want to prefer charges against this man?"

"Who me? Naw." He called Crole a particularly vile name and spat afterwards.

"Okay, Connely," said Jorgens. "But if you want to keep on the safe side of the law, you'd better show yourself a little more often to the Parole Board. Now get out."

Hardboiled Connely shuffled out of headquarters. A taxi was standing at the curb. He got in and growled an address.

"Right, sir," said George Scavillo, throwing on the meter.

Captain Jorgens said not a word until he was positive that Connely was clear of the building, then he turned to the private detective.

"How'd I do?" he asked.

Simon Crole grinned approvingly. "Swell, Captain. You took the cue better than I hoped for."

"Humm! It's time you explained things. Come into my office."

They followed him in. Crole said: "My operator's had a tough time, Captain. So have I, though in a different way. How's for a drink." He smiled his surprised smile.

After the captain had complied with the formalities, he said: "All right. I'm listening."

Simon Crole rolled a cigarette. After a long inhalation he said: "Two guys came into the Casino just as we were leaving. They were evidently expected by someone inside the club. I had Esther tail them when they left. She followed them to my office. They were there while I was down on Nineteenth street talking with you, or about that time."

Jorgens chewed morosely on his cigar. "Huh," he grunted.

"I don't know what they did there, but they did something. She tailed them some more and finally got to Eighty-seventh street. They're wise by this time and grab her when she starts to look the joint over from the outside."

Crole inhaled slowly. "I'm tipped by the cab driver when

Esther failed to return, and I goes down there breathing fire. Connely tried to give me an argument, but I spiked that at the beginning. I found my op tied up. Connely had busted her in the cheek. So I busted Connely."

Captain Jorgens frowned. "But what has all this to do with your wild yammering out front of the sergeant's desk."

"The captain," said Esther, trying in vain to fasten the torn shoulder straps of her dress, "has well expressed my own thoughts."

Simon Crole blinked at the flat cigarette in his fingers. "Just a little missionary work," he said, "to help the cause. Nothing like discord and suspicion to break up a crooked organization."

"You mean," said Captain Jorgens, "that through Hardboiled Connely . . . ?"

"The same. Connely will squeal to those hood friends of his. He'll wise them to what I said about the fat man who runs the gambling joint. I know how the minds of those mobsters work. Once they get to wondering about the man above them, and doubting him, they'll begin to do a little serious thinking. And when men of this type begin to think—action follows."

The lidded eyes of the police captain were thoughtful. "Sometimes this is the best way, Simon."

"That's the way I figure. And here's the angle. Larkin, Nicky Lombardo and Gat O'Brien all worked for the same man. Maybe there were others. I don't know."

Jorgens nodded heavily. "Go on," he said.

Crole went on. "Does this man protect Larkin when he gets into a jam? No. Does he forgive Gat O'Brien when he made a slight error which I claim was not his fault? No. He's so scared that he can't trust anybody. Given time he'll hire outside punks to rub out these two hoods who fixed O'Brien tonight. They've got plenty on him. And through these two men we'll get at him —and all because of his desperate, craven fear of everybody around him."

18

THE PINCH

SIMON CROLE, still in evening dress, but minus his hat, felt something hard press into his side. He had taken Esther home and returned to his apartment when August Fweeble and the man wearing the purple tie accosted him in the apartment lobby.

"Gus," said Crole, "you know that isn't nice—prodding me with a gun that way."

The jaunty little man smiled crookedly. His voice was brittle and wholly unlike that of the meek man who had seemed so harmless, "You're coming with us, Crole. Down to your office. There'll be others down there waiting for us. We ought to have a nice, friendly session."

"And just who are these others, Gus?"

"You'll see when we get there."

Crole thought this over. "Got time to go up to my apartment and have a drink?"

"No," said Fweeble. "Get moving. I've waited up most of the night trying to get you. You're smart, Crole. Damned smart. But you tripped up finally."

Wedged between the two men, Crole was driven rapidly downtown in Fweeble's roadster. He addressed the man on his right. "How's things at the National City?"

The man wearing the purple tie said: "Pretty. Couldn't be better."

Crole turned to Fweeble. "This guy work for you, Gus?"

"Why not? He's a good man."

"You guys bank detectives?"

"Nope. Private agency like your own—only straight."

The agency man yawned. "I hate to see you mixed up in this pinch, Gus. You know, I kinda like you, as I remarked several times before. So don't take it too hard if I pull a fast one on you."

Crole felt the gun prod his right ribs. He spoke patiently to the jaunty little man. "I'm not planning to run out on you, Gus, so tell this bright boy next to me to quit shoving that gun against my ribs. Tell him to save it till he meets the right guy."

They left the machine at the building's entrance.

"Sorry," apologized Crole, "about the elevator service. They go dead after midnight. Well, maybe the walk will do us good. It won't be the first time I've climbed these old stairs."

He arrived at the seventh floor puffing slightly. At the end of the hall, clustered around the entrance to his office, Simon Crole saw six men. Four of them were in police uniforms. And conspicuous among them was Lieutenant Bemus.

"What a pleasant surprise," observed Crole, surveying the hall filled with men. He unlocked the door and passed inside, switched on the lights and grinned at the eight men as they entered one behind the other.

"Evening, Judge Chadwick. Heard you were out of town. And the district attorney. Minifie, I'm glad to welcome you. Bemus, you're as welcome as the itch. Keep your handcuffs in your pocket. You'll never use them on me."

He backed away from the doorway and indicated chairs, which none accepted. Slowly he rolled a cigarette and sat down on his secretary's desk. "Well," he said, "let's hear all about it, gentlemen. You've certainly come out in force. All you need is a machine gun and you'd be a complete squad."

Judge Chadwick broke the silence. "I believe it was understood that I was to make the first charge," he stated.

The others nodded. Chadwick continued. "I have here a statement," he began, taking a folded sheet of paper from his pocket, "that was delivered to me in person by a man whose name I will not mention. This statement was apparently written by a gangster who accused my son of shooting a police officer named Malloy. Subsequent investigation proves that it was not written by this gangster, but in the office where we are now gathered."

Simon Crole nodded complacently. "Excellent. Is that the original draft, Judge, or, let us say, a photostatic copy?"

"It's the original draft."

"It was my impression," began Crole, staring hard at the jurist, "that the original draft was in the hands of . . ."

"Your impressions scarcely matter," said Chadwick, coldly.

"We believe this statement was typed in this office. Do you deny it?"

Simon Crole saw in an instant where all this was leading. And he felt keenly against the judge being made an instrument in the frame. "Swell," he said. "There's two typewriters in the office. Compare the type."

One of the cops took specimen sentences from both machines and compared them with Nicky Lombardo's statement. "This one's it," he pointed. "No use searching further."

Bemus sneered craftily. "That's what I thought."

District Attorney Minifie spoke for the first time. "Crole, you have never explained to my satisfaction your reason for being in Charles Jensen's apartment at or about the time he was . . . ah, hung."

"Nor why he rented the place today through one of his operators," added Bemus.

"Bemus," said Crole. "I didn't think you would ever find it out. All right. I rented the apartment through someone else. Is that a crime? Now ask me something more."

"Sure. Where did you get the gun Fweeble's operator took from you, and later recovered by our office?"

"Was it the actual gun used to kill Malloy?" asked Crole.

"You know it was."

"I wasn't sure. Well, I paid seven bucks for that gun at a loan broker's on Main street."

"But how," asked the district attorney, "did you come to go there for it in the first place."

Simon Crole rubbed his bald head. "I forget how it was," he said.

The district attorney smiled pityingly. "Well, Crole, it looks as if we've got two counts right there. I believe you, yourself, killed Charles Jensen. You figured he had the balance of the money not yet recovered for the bank. You also figured that since you reported the crime you would not be suspected."

"You really think that, Minifie?"

"I'm telling you, Crole, how it appears to me."

Crole's eyebrows lifted. "And you, Judge Chadwick?"

"I refuse to commit myself."

"And you, Fweeble?"

"Well now," hedged Fweeble.

"Don't stall," said Crole. "Follow your gentlemanly instincts and tell these guys what you know. Tell them how you drove me to the Biltmore that night, and how we got away from the Homicide man who was tailing us. Tell them how we had dinner that evening, and what time we left the hotel."

"Is this true, Fweeble?" snapped the D. A. crossly.

Gus Fweeble nodded. "We were together up to a half hour or so before he phoned the police."

Crole said: "There goes your murder charge. As for this typewriter one of my ops bought it. He got it on a certain day long after Judge Chadwick received the statement he tells about. I have a receipt from the dealer to prove it. If you care to examine . . ."

The phone rang sharply. Crole pushed the receiver against his ear. "Simon Crole, speaking," he said.

George Scavillo's voice came over the wire. "I took that guy back to Eighty-seventh street. There was two other guys waiting for him on the corner."

"Thanks." He hung up.

"Who was that?" asked Minifie.

"One of my ops reporting in."

The district attorney was not altogether happy. "Your explanations are all too glib, Crole. I'm going to search your office whether you like it or not. I've had a pretty good tip that you're mixed up in one murder—probably two. Lieutenant Bemus, you and your men go over these rooms thoroughly."

Crole's eyes narrowed. "Not without a warrant, Mr. District Attorney."

"The order stands as I gave it. Go ahead, Bemus."

There was a queer silence as the police ransacked the place. A red-faced cop found it—a length of lead pipe.

"Where'd you discover this?" asked the district attorney.

"In the cupboard behind a filing cabinet."

Bemus crossed the room in three swift strides. "Lead pipe, did you say? Look! There's blood on it, and human hairs." His lips twisted crookedly. "I'm beginning to see light. Gat O'Brien was bumped off only a few hours ago. The medical examiner reported that he had been struck over the head with a lead pipe. This can be easily proven, the hair and blood checked." He turned grimly on the private detective. "Maybe you've got a smart come-back for this, eh?"

Crole shook his head sadly. "No, I haven't."

The police officer's smile was exultant. "I thought not. We've got you cold on this one, you bald-headed hippo. You bit off more than you could chew. This finishes you and your private detective racket."

He turned to the district attorney. "I'll take this pipe down and put one of our experts to work on it. Crole, you're under arrest, charged with murder." Then to his men. "Take him down to headquarters."

District Attorney Minifie was frowning thoughtfully after Bemus had left. His eyes were on the big detective sitting calmly on the desk. "How do you feel now, Crole?"

Simon Crole's face was expressionless. "I was wondering, Mr. District Attorney, how *you'll* feel when the newspapers give you the horselaugh."

"That's not probable."

Crole resumed. "I credit you with a fair amount of brains, or you wouldn't be holding down your present job. But, Minifie, whether you'll admit it or not, you're afraid of pressure from above. Somebody's got to take the rap for these killings. Public opinion demands it. But you're making a mistake—a serious mistake—in picking me for the goat. Go ahead. Place me under arrest and see how far you'll get."

"That's exactly what I'm doing, Crole."

"Could I have a word with Gus Fweeble in private, before you slip on the bracelets?"

"Make it short. I'm tired of hanging around."

In his private office Crole said to the other agency man: "Gus, you're all wet in your suspicions, as you'll find out later. You're after the money Jensen got away with. All right. I'll see that you get it."

The jaunty little man regarded Crole sharply. "Where is it?"

"Believe it or not, Gus, the police have it—Captain Jorgens to be exact, but us three are the only ones who know it. Play along with me, you and your friend with the purple tie, and I'll see that your agency doesn't lose caste."

"What's on your mind?"

"I want you to go to a certain address. My op, Matt Ridley

.will be there. Tell him how things stack up." He looked at his watch. "The place is across from the building where Schilling has his office. Can see into it swell. Bemus will go to headquarters with the chunk of pipe. Then he'll make a phone call. I'm playing a hunch that the fat boy who controls things in this city will burn up the streets getting down to his office. Maybe you'll see him. Will you do this for me?"

"I don't quite get the point you're imperfectly explaining."

"But you will, Gus." He wrote the name of the building, its location and the office number on a piece of paper. "Here's the dope. You still able to make a pinch?"

"I got *you*, didn't I?"

"Yes, you got me. But I'm not tough. You may have a job on your hands. There's two hoods. I expect them to be there in a certain man's office. Grab them when they come out. They're important."

"How much longer is this confab going to continue," growled Minifie, petulantly.

"Half a minute," called back Crole. Then to Fweeble. "I was gonna make this pinch myself, but you see how it is."

"Who are these hoods you tell about?"

"They're the answer to a policeman's prayer. Bring them in, Gus, and you'll cover yourself with glory. Luck to you."

Gus Fweeble nodded. "This isn't by any chance the fast one you mentioned earlier?"

"You should have laid your cards on the table in the first place, Gus. You and your wife are out a big bunch of dough."

"The D. A. and Mark gave me a bum steer. I believed everything they told me, till Bemus brought out that chunk of lead pipe. That was too much. I'll see you later—Simon."

"Swell, Gus. I knew you was regular, even if you was working with the other side."

Hardboiled Connely, speaking from the side of his mouth, said: "So this big guy horns in. He was tough and mean. He beats the hell out of me, springs the jane and takes me down to headquarters."

"What'd he look like," said Willie.

"He looked like bad news. Bald-headed, white shirt and tux.

But he wasn't no dick. In front of the sarge's desk he blew off his mouth in front of Jorgens. Said he was a friend of O'Brien's. Said he was looking for you two guys for bumping him off. Oh, he had your number all right. Said he got it from the fat guy who runs the Casino."

"The hell he did," said Willie, quietly.

"That fat slob," growled Dutch Peters, "turned us in."

Willie's slow-working mind revolved painfully. "The Chief ratted on us, Dutch. Do you get it? He's through with us— same as he got through with Larkin and O'Brien and Strangler, and a lot of other guys. That big guy with the bald head must be a new punk from out of town. Geez, can yuh tie that. We've been crossed."

"You telling me, Willie? Hell, I could see this comin' a long time ago. You heard me shoot off my mouth tonight . . ."

"Yeah," said Willie, "and I snapped at yuh." He sighed, rubbed his lips, and made queer sounds in his throat. His sallow face was like a death mask. A long, ugly word puffed his lips out. "I didn't think he'd do this—to me. I didn't think it."

"Well, let's go," said Dutch.

Connely said: "Not me. I'm out. This is *your* party. I'm fixing me an alibi."

Dutch Peters spat. "How about it, Willie. Are you with me, or do I go alone?"

"Where you headed for?"

"I'm headed for where I can find that fat guy. He's got a lot to explain to me."

Willie said ominously: "I'll handle this, Dutch. He'll do his explaining to me—as if it would do him any good. I'm sorry as hell for the guy who owns that office where we planted the lead pipe."

"We was paid for that plant, wasn't we?"

Willie said as if he hadn't heard, "The fat guy fixes things so that a private dick gets hooked on framed evidence. Then he brings in some outside punk to turn the heat on us so we can't rat on him. Which leaves him safe and sitting pretty."

"Hell," growled Dutch Peters. "What we waiting for?"

"I was trying to get it straight in my mind," said Willie.

19

THE SCOURGE OF FEAR

THE bell rang ten seconds after the light had been switched off. Mark Schilling felt suddenly cold. He slid his feet from under the sheets and snapped on the table lamp. His fat jowls quivered as he spoke into the mouthpiece. "Hello!"

"Everything's fixed," said the voice of Lieutenant Bemus. "We copped the dick shortly after two o'clock and he's down at the D. A.'s office. We may have trouble with the first two charges. That guy's smart. Too damned smart. But the third charge . . ."

"No, no," said the fat man. "Not over the phone. Come up to my house . . . change that. Come to my office. I can think better there. I'll get dressed and go right down."

"Can't get away. I . . ."

"Come down to my office, I said." He hung up. Cleared his throat and began to dress. "That private dick," he told himself, softly, "had me scared. I've got a feeling he's going to be hard to handle in court. He'll squawk with the help of his lawyer. But I'm ready for the investigation."

He knotted his tie, pulled on his coat, breathed heavily and rang for his private car. From a wall safe he took a huge wad of bills. Never could tell when he'd need a little hush money to silence certain people. But he'd smash this private dick if it was the last thing he ever did.

He was afraid, was Mark Schilling. Deathly afraid. "I'm all right," he reassured himself as he waddled out to the car purring at the curb. "I'm protected. They can't do nothing to me. My system will take care of everything. Bemus knows what he's doing. I'll put some more pressure on the D. A. He'll work hard for a conviction. Geez, I'm sweating."

His chair creaked protestingly as he eased his gross bulk into it. There. That was better. Now he could think. Could keep his fingers on the pulse of things. How quiet it was. He looked at his watch. Half past three.

With the tips of his fingers he tapped nervously against the blotter. Self-protection was the only way out. That had been a smart trick to give Chadwick the original of the photostat copy.

It meant the loss of his hold on the judge, but there were other ways of regaining it later on. He wouldn't worry about the judge right now. His greatest threat was that bald-headed dick with the sly, surprised smile.

The eyes of the fat man became furtive. He tried to twist his head on the pillars of fat holding it up. He had to twist the whole upper part of his body. Did he hear feet on the stairs?

How quiet it was. He took a mauve handkerchief from his breast pocket and mopped his forehead. He listened again. There was no sound but the quickened beat of his heart.

He thought, for no reason at all, of Charles Jensen. He saw him hanging at the end of the rope, swaying slightly from the touch of the Medical Examiner's hands. He heard again, as had Simon Crole, the mournful howl forced from the mouth of the corpse.

He forced the gruesome picture from his mind. "If Bemus," he promised himself, "handles this right, I'll see that he gets the Captaincy of the Eleventh Precinct. It'll be worth it. If that chunk of lead pipe isn't enough, I'll buy some witnesses. The pay-off on those gravel contracts will handle everything. I don't have to worry. I don't . . ."

This time he really heard a sound in the hall. He breathed stertoriously as he got to his feet and waddled to the door. He called from inside. "Who is it?"

"Bemus."

"Ah, come in, Lieutenant. Everything all right?" The query was almost a whine. "There hasn't been any slip-up . . ."

Bemus smiled craftily. "Everything's shaping up grand. We've got that bald-headed dick on ice, Mark. It'll be a cinch. If you want to put out some jack, there's that woman that runs the joint where O'Brien roomed. A couple of hundred bucks and she'd swear away the life of her own brother."

Mark Schilling was pleased. He felt the load slip from his shoulders. "We'll take care of her, Mike. We'll have an iron-clad case of this before we're through."

Bemus said: "It'll take some fixing, though."

"You can handle it, can't you?"

"Oh, sure. But where do I get off . . .?"

"I was getting to that," said the fat man, resuming his seat behind the desk. "On Monday I'll go down and see the Commissioner. The police budget comes up next week. He wants it increased. I can fix that part of it. Don't worry, I'll see that you're into the Eleventh Precinct with a captain's rating. How's that?"

Bemus nodded. "Nothing else to report, Mark. Got to get back to headquarters to get in on the first hearing. I'll keep you informed."

"You do that, Mike," smiled the fat man. "And I'll see that you're taken care of. I mean that. I'll certainly see that you're taken care of."

As Bemus emerged to the street after leisurely walking down the stairs, he realized with a sudden shock that his customary caution had deserted him. He cursed his own stupidity.

Coming along the walk towards him were three men. They made no move to stop him, but in passing, one of them spoke. It was Crole's operator, Matt Ridley.

"H'are yuh, Bemus? Out kinda late, aren't you?"

Bemus muttered something unintelligible and moved on. From over his shoulder he looked back. The three men had passed the entrance to the Commercial building and were headed farther uptown.

At ten minutes to four, Mark Schilling got to his feet; thought of something and sat down again. From his pocket he took the small leather-bound book. Holding a pencil in his pudgy fingers he drew a line through a name—the name was O'Brien.

There was another name beneath, recently added to the list—Simon Crole. He placed a question mark at the end of it, and returned the book to his pocket. In the act of getting up a second time, he paused, swung sideways. He hadn't heard a sound. But the door was slowly opening.

Willie Stevens came in. Crowding close behind him was Dutch Peters.

"Close the door, Dutch," ordered Willie. His hands were thrust deep in the side pockets of his coat.

Mark Schilling's pale eyes glazed with the fear he had felt only a short time before. There was something in Willie's behavior that sent icy tremors racing along his spine. He tried to appear casual.

"Hello, Willie. What are you doing down in the building at this hour? I didn't send for you."

"No," said Willie. His eyes seemed to focus on a point above the fat man's head. "Me and Dutch came here after we found out you wasn't home or at the Casino."

"I see. Well?" he coughed nervously.

Willie said: "So you're through with us, huh? Got no more use for a couple of punks like me and Dutch. Yuh got rid of Larkin, Strangler, and O'Brien, Now it's our turn. The guy you ratted to come to our place on Eighty-seventh street. He spilled Connely and his guts all over the place. He said you . . ."

Schilling's face became pasty. "Willie, you're crazy!"

Willie's voice was a dull monotone. "Sure, I'm crazy. I'm so crazy, Schilling, that I'm gonna add another murder to my string. What do you think of that?"

The fat man took out a thick roll of bills. "You boys are good," he said, his voice trembling. "I know what you're after. You're shaking me down for more money. That's okay, too. You deserve it. How much this time?"

"We'll take it all," snarled Dutch Peters.

"Wait," said Willie. "This is gonna be good, Dutch. Watch him sweat." His right hand withdrew slowly from his coat pocket. The overhead light caught and reflected the dull blue of the automatic's snub-nose. "Ain't this good, Dutch?"

Mark Schilling squirmed uneasily in his chair. It creaked beneath the shifting weight of his gross body. Cold sweat jumped out on his forehead. Fear brought on a faint nausea. A thin stream of spittle ran down from his lips and lost itself in the folds beneath his chin.

"Before God," he pleaded, "I was playing safe with you, Willie. You've got to believe me. Somebody lied to you. Listen, you can't do this. You're my number one man since . . . since Strangler went away. Look? I'll pay you plenty if you're sore about . . . See? I got it with me . . . lots of good, government notes—maybe thirty grand, Willie."

The eyes of Willie Stevens were like chunks of burnished

metal. His lips were frozen into a hypnotic grin void of all mirth. His heart was hot with sullen rage. His soul—Willie Stevens had no soul at that moment.

In a cold, unemotional voice he began to speak. His words were cruel, biting and damningly true in all essentials but one. But he didn't know that this one thing wasn't true.

Schilling tried to tell him, but Willie cut him off sharply and went on with his scathing indictment. Willie was mad—mad as only a man with a slow-working brain becomes mad. And this madness seemed to burn with brighter intensity as the hot words spewed from his lips. Schilling broke in with a hoarse babble.

The gun's explosion cut him off sharply. A long spear of flame stabbed outward from the snub-nosed automatic.

Shocked, numbed surprise filled the pale eyes of the fat man behind the desk. Slowly, reluctantly, as if mortally afraid of what they might see, those pale eyes drifted from the faintly smoking gun in Willie's hand to the smear of scarlet darkening his shirt front.

He knew, then, in the vortex of pain twinges, how other men had felt when the shadow of death was upon them. He could still see the drifting smoke curl hanging in the air. It seemed ages since the explosion had dinned his ears.

He tried to move. He tried to keep himself from sinking into oblivion. Oddly enough, it seemed to him that his body was like a punctured balloon, collapsing slowly into huge folds that spread crazily over chair, desk and the entire room.

His pudgy, dimpled hands were before him on the desk blotter. They seemed no part of him. They were like the penholder, the blotter or the ashtray. His eyes strayed up from his hands. Willie's gun arm was extended. But he was a long distance away, faint and indistinct like something dimly seen through fog tendrils.

The fat man knew he was falling. And there was nothing he could do about it. His mountainous body slumped forward against the desk edge, was exerting pressure against the chair. The chair was slipping backwards on its casters.

He tried to grip the desk with his fingers and so bring his body upward so he could lean back in his chair. His muscles responded, tightened. His pudgy fingers pressed down. Hard.

And all they succeeded in doing was to press two buttons beneath the blotter. He knew that was not what he intended. He was sure of it for he did not want the wall panels to open.

Yet, they were opening on their silent hinges. The room was contracting swiftly. Objects were no longer miles away, half lost in a fog. They were sharp and distinct. Willie was only a few feet away. His gun arm was sweeping around in a half circle.

The fat man's eyes were opaque. For some reason, not clear to himself, he was not surprised at what he saw. It seemed, in a way, perfectly natural. In the opening beyond the panel stood two men, one of them in the uniform of a captain of the police. The other was Simon Crole.

The sudden uproar of guns crashed against his ears like physical blows. His lips puffed out. A sound like a choked snore issued from his throat. The chair jerked suddenly backward. He fell—slowly, in a grotesque, pulsing heap of flesh.

The telephone on the district attorney's desk made noisy clamor. Minifie thrust the receiver against his ear. "Hello. Who? Crole? What do you want of him? You can give me the message. You won't? Then it's too bad. Oh, you want Captain Jorgens, then?" He thrust the instrument across the desk. "Take it, Captain."

"Yeah," said Jorgens. "Oh, Ridley. Go ahead."

Matt's voice crackled. "Listen, Captain. I'm down at the Commerce building. Schilling's place is all lit up. Bemus was just up to see him. He's been there before. There's something funny going on. Two men, mean looking guys, just went in the building. There ain't another light in the place except in Schilling's office. You'd better get down here if you want to nail them for questioning. Bring Simon with you."

Jorgens took the cigar from between his teeth. "What is this, Ridley—a trick?"

"Do like I tell you. I'll be inside. Fweeble and his man are here at the side entrance. I'm guarding the front. I think these are the guys what bumped off O'Brien. Hurry!"

Captain Jorgens slammed the receiver to its hook. "Come on, Simon," he said to the private detective, jerking his thumb towards the door. "It's your op. He's a little excited about something."

"You can't do this," protested the district attorney. "Crole's under arrest."

Jorgens moistened his lips. "Yeah? But he's under my care. With me he goes. I'll be responsible."

Minifie jumped to his feet. "Captain Jorgens, I order . . ."

Jorgens broke in. "Your job is to prosecute. Mine is to make arrests. Make a move to stop me or Simon Crole, and I'll make it damned hot for you. You've interfered long enough. I'm sick of running around in circles. Come on, Simon."

For once the police car snaked up to the front of a building without any wailing of siren.

"Damn that Bemus," muttered the police Captain. "I'll know what to do with him . . ."

"Upstairs," said Crole. "Ah, here's Matt. Listen, the Captain and I will go up. You stay below . . ."

They pushed past the protesting operator and climbed the stairs. A light gleamed through the glass panel on Schilling's door. The office of the dentist was on their left. That of the contractor on their right. They could hear a low monotone of a voice, indistinct and blurred.

Crole took out a bunch of skeleton keys. He tried them one by one on the dentist's door. No luck. He turned to the lock of the contractor's office. The lock bolt slipped back. They slid inside and left the door open.

They moved close to the wall adjoining Schilling's office. The voices of the men reached them quite distinctly.

"Pray," said a voice that was not Schilling's. "Or maybe you've forgotten how—same as you've forgotten all the poor guys you framed into the big house when you figured they was too dangerous to be in your mob any longer."

"I never framed anybody," they heard the fat man scream.

Accusations and answers.

"You've done worse," said the first voice. "You let Larkin take his rap without furnishing a mouthpiece. You had me and Dutch bump off Strangler because Jensen croaked on him, and there wasn't any coin in sight. You paid us to bump off O'Brien, and to frame this guy with a chunk of lead pipe. I could forget all that, but I can't forget you ratting on us tonight, and . . ."

"Who said I ratted on you?"

"Big guy in evening clothes. Bald-headed. Scar on his . . ."

Simon Crole felt suddenly uneasy. Captain Jorgens was pawing at the wall in hopes of finding the panel that opened.

"Oh God!" came the voice of Schilling. "Don't believe that dick. Willie! Don't! Can't you see? It's a trick. You're being used to . . . put up that gun. You've got to believe me. I wouldn't cross you, Willie . . ."

The ominous crack of the gun caused both men to draw back from the wall. Crole's lips twisted into their smile of surprise. It was up to the police officer to take charge now.

Jorgen's hand moved to his hip pocket. As it emerged gripped hard on a police .38 special, the wall in front of them opened on its silent hinges.

Crole saw the fat man stare at him stupidly, his eyes glazed, his lips puffed out. He saw also the sharp features of the sallow-faced man, Willie Stevens. Saw the gun arm of Stevens arch in a half circle.

The .38 special filled the room with thunder. Willie Stevens cursed savagely. His automatic spat twice. His right wrist started to bleed. He shifted his gun. Dutch Peters, his back to the wall fired as the police captain barged through the opening. The bullet caught Jorgens in the shoulder and spun him around.

Willie's left hand was getting a firm grip on the automatic. Simon Crole moved fast. He had no gun—nothing but his hands. He slapped Willie's gun upward. Bullets, three of them, bit into the ceiling. Crole's second hand curved outward—bunched into a hard fist.

Willie twisted slightly. The blow struck him glancingly beneath the ear. He fell sprawling, his back to Schilling's desk. A sickly grin spread over his face. He fired again. The bullet seared hotly across the calf of Crole's leg. Then his grin was snuffed out, as the big body of the agency man smothered him against the floor. He tried to jam the snub-nosed gun against the big body. A hand pawed his face, gripped it, raised it till his neck almost cracked, then thrust it down hard. The back of his head smacked against the desk. The automatic slipped from his fingers.

Simon Crole grabbed it. "Get up," he said. "Stand with your face to the wall." He leaned against the desk and watched the man face the wall as commanded. He turned his head sideways. Jorgens was standing in the doorway, rich curses dribbling from his lips. Crole could hear the feet of the second man pounding down the stairs.

Then from the well of the stairway he heard a gun blast, a faint yelp, then silence.

"You curse swell," said Crole. "But it ain't doing you no good. How about some metal on this guy's wrists. Don't worry about the one who got away. Matt will nail him without trouble."

"I got hit," said Jorgens, "in the shoulder." He took a pair of steel bracelets from his pocket and linked Willie to a chair arm. "Sit down," he said. "Simon, call the D. A. Is the fat man still alive? That's a break. Maybe we can get him to talk."

Crole went out into the hall. Matt Ridley, grinning sheepishly was coming up the last flight of stairs. "I fell down," he said, "ducking that guy's bullet. I didn't have no gun. But that other dick and his man Friday grabbed him at the side door."

Crole said: "Matt, you *would* fall down—or something." He called down the stair well. "Gus. Bring that guy up." He went back to Schilling's desk and picked up the phone. "Office of the district attorney. Hello, Minifie? Simon Crole. There's been a little shooting . . . yeah, Mark Schilling's office. Jorgens says to give you a ring in case you'd like to straighten out some of the kinks in your thinking."

He sighed and rubbed his bald head. "Who we got? You'd be surprised."

His eyes became gloomy. "Listen, Mr. District Attorney. There are times in your official career when you act like a spoiled child. I keep telling you I didn't kill Jensen or O'Brien. You got proof? Listen, keep that proof under lock and key. If the newshawks ever get hold of it, you're sunk. Whatever it is they do to dumb district attorneys they'll do that to you. G'bye."

"It seems," said Jorgens, wincing at the pain in his shoulder, "that Minifie doubts your word?"

Crole got out tobacco sack and papers. "Captain," he said,

"long after all this blows over, he'll be accusing me of suppressing evidence, collecting huge fees, hiding important witnesses . . ."

"Simon," said Captain Jorgens. "I know damn well you'll never tell all you know. Whatever the D. A.'s shortcomings, he'll be right in accusing you of these things you said he would."

Simon Crole lighted his cigarette, crossed to the window, stared down the long rows of lights of the early morning streets and saw the red lights of the police cars long before their screaming sirens announced their swift coming. He sighed, and said peevishly: "Captain, I never knew a man so eternally and everlastingly suspicious of his fellow men . . ."

"Damn the fellow men part, Simon. I'm referring directly to you."

"Yeah?" said Crole. "I heard you the first time.

20

SIMON COLLECTS

TRAILING a long streamer announcing the completion of a brand new sub-division, a fat blimp chugged across the Sunday morning sky above the coastal city that people from the east called an upstart that was striving desperately to be metropolitan.

District Attorney Minifie sat behind his desk fussing importantly. Around the desk were grouped an interesting collection of faces. The hands of the clock on the wall registered eleven.

Judge Chadwick sat on one side, his lean face inscrutable. Next to him in order were Fweeble, the man with the purple tie, Ridley, Bemus and Jorgens. Crole sat a little removed from the rest, a look of boredom on his round face.

Minifie frowned. "Lieutenant Bemus," he began. "What was your connection with Mark Schilling."

"None at all."

"Were you ever in his office?"

"No. Why should I go there?"

"Why indeed. I wish I knew. Matt Ridley, did you see Bemus in Schilling's office?"

"Once I tailed him into the dentist's office that connects with Schilling's by a small panel that opens. Early this morning I saw him there from a window across the street. Fweeble was with me at the time. We also, saw him leave the building."

"Was this before or after Crole's arrest?"

"After."

"I believe, Captain Jorgens," said the district attorney, dryly, "that the leak in official headquarters can easily be traced to this police officer. I'd suggest he be detained for further investigation."

"You've got nothing on me!" shouted Bemus, angrily, half rising.

Jorgens yanked his fellow officer back to the chair. "Close your trap, Bemus. You'll find out later whether we've got anything on you."

The district attorney resumed. "Simon Crole," he said. "The verbal report of Captain Jorgens clears you of any murder charges my office may have erroneously brought against your name. But there are several points that will have to be cleared up. The money, believed to be in Jensen's possession at the time of his death, has never been recovered. Being a large sum it is important . . ."

"There's a package on your desk," said Crole. "Open it up."

"It's already been opened," said Jorgens. "I opened it myself in the presence of two witnesses. Inside was a black cash box, sealed tightly all around its edges with heavy wax. The box itself was wrapped in oil-silk paper, with coarse wrapping paper covering that. In the box when we opened it was a hundred and five thousand dollars."

"Where did you get this box, Captain?"

"Simon Crole."

"And you, Crole?"

"Jensen's apartment. I rented it after the police got through pawing around. I figured the money was still there. I figured that Jensen was being tortured so that he would reveal the hiding place of the money. But owing to a slight accident, he quit breathing before his hangman could do anything about it."

"What made you think that?"

"Call it a hunch. The reasoning was involved, so we'll pass over it. Obviously, the place to look for it was the one spot in the apartment overlooked by the police. I found it—on the bottom of an aquarium tank under two inches of sand."

Minifie nodded, but it was apparent to everyone that he was not altogether satisfied. "There's one point more," he went on "The others will come up with the trial of Schilling's gunmen. You knew, Simon Crole, that Mark died in the hospital at eight this morning?"

"I heard he died, yes."

"What you didn't hear, Crole, was his opinion of you and the devious ways of your agency."

"No, I didn't hear that part. It must have been good."

"Schilling said," went on the district attorney, reading from a slip of paper; "I don't suppose I should howl because a couple of my rats turned on me. Maybe I had it coming. The racket was good while it lasted. But you can tell the city prosecutor that there's only one smart dick in the city, and he's a private detective. You can also add this to my will. For fees lost through my own interference, the sum of four-thousand, five-hundred dollars will be paid to Simon Crole, the only man who ever out-guessed Mark Schilling."

"I'd like to thank Mark for thinking of me," said Crole. "But I don't want his money. In a way I feel responsible for his sudden death."

"Then you won't take it?" asked the district attorney.

"Eh? You confuse mental reservations, Minifie, with hard facts. Sure, I'll take the fee. Maybe I earned it, maybe I didn't. But that's nobody's business but my own." He yawned. "I've been up all night. So have you. If this preliminary hearing is finished, I'll take myself home and get some sleep."

District Attorney Minifie shrugged. "I guess there's nothing more to discuss right now," he said. "As a matter of fact I'll be glad to get rid of you, Crole. You get on my nerves."

Crole lunged to his feet. His leg hurt where Willie's bullet had singed the flesh. He hobbled over to where his operator was getting up from a chair. "Listen, Matt. This'll be all for now. On Monday you can close up your office and get rid of the furniture. If you talk hard and fast enough to the building superintendent, you might get a rebate on the month's rent you paid. You can try, anyway."

"Sure, boss. I'll see what I can do. Anything else?"

"No. Go home and go to bed."

"Who, me? Say, I should waste my life sleeping. I'm going down to the Rivoli. They tell me they's a swell crook picture being shown."

"Nerts," sighed Crole.

He button-holed August Fweeble. "Gus," he whispered. "Get whatever's left of the bank money from the district attorney." He grinned ruefully. "I'm sure gonna miss you and your Missus as clients. Them fees you paid me cost you plenty. What exactly was your idea, anyhow?"

"Poor guesswork on my part, Simon. I followed a man named King to your office. I knew he was a friend of Larkin's. I had hoped to get a line on the money through him. He led me to you and I stuck to you hoping for a break that would prove you were implicated. But don't worry about the fees. I'm not. The bank pays all expenses."

"Umm. Well, remember me to Mrs. Fweeble. She played her part swell. She took me in like nobody ever did before."

Fweeble grinned. "The old girl is good," he said. "Listen, Simon, if you're ever up Denver way, look me up. I'm with the International Agency."

Crole wagged his bald head sadly. "Me," he said, "I never get out of this town. Would you believe it, the damn place is growing just like New York. Some day, if I grow with it, I'm gonna be one of the big shots with hundreds of operators."

The eyes of the jaunty little man twinkled. "From what I've seen, heard and guessed, you're doing pretty well as it is. You seem to have the knack of collecting from everybody."

"Fees," scoffed the private detective. "I never give them a thought. I make 'em high, and when people pay, everything's jake. I'm having a swell time. Good food, excellent liquor, and friendly with everybody—well, the police are a little difficult at times. But I get by with them. It's a grand way to make a living. Will I see you again before you go back to Denver?"

"I'll drop into your office tomorrow."

"Swell. I'll mix you the perfect drink. One of my women operators, and she was regular before she hooked up with the County, is crazy about this drink. In fact she told me once that the idea back of it was her own. But Esther is a lawyer, so I don't believe or disbelieve. She calls her drink an Alexander. One part gin, one part . . ."

Gus Fweeble chuckled. "I've had that drink in New Orleans, in Chicago, in Milwaukee . . ."

"Let it pass," said Crole. "Anyhow, it's Esther's story, and she's gonna stick to it, believe me." He turned away. "See you tomorrow, Gus," he called over his shoulder.

He looked around the room. Except for Judge Chadwick, standing alone by an open window, the room was empty. He limped across the room to the open window. "Hello, Judge," he said.

Judge Chadwick turned slowly. There were hollows beneath his eyes. His face was haggard with suffering. "Simon," he said. "I'm an older man than you are. My life has always run in a narrow groove. I haven't had your experience. I've judged crooks, gangsters and human scum from the safety of my court bench."

Crole said: "Yeah, I know all that. You found it hard to believe that I was still working for your interests. You got through the first part of it fine. I knew what was in your mind when you canned me from the job at your house."

He paused for a moment. "I knew how you felt regarding Gordon. I talked with that boy of yours. I got the whole story from him. He's okay. He needs something to interest him. He needs work. Get him a job—any kind of a job. He thinks you're pretty fine."

A faint smile spread over the jurist's face. "I'm glad to hear that, Simon."

"That statement, Judge, you brought up in my office. Was it really the original?"

"It was, and it's been destroyed. Schilling had a sudden change of heart. He brought it to me and told me, confidentially, that the whole thing originated in your office. I tried not to believe him even after the machine on which it was written was found exactly where he told me it would be found."

"You're satisfied, Judge, that . . ."

"I received your bill," broke in the judge, "and tore it up. You will make out another one immediately. The fee, Simon, will be ten thousand dollars."

Simon Crole swallowed heavily. "Too much."

"Don't argue with an old man, Simon. Where's my boy?"

"Is your car on the street?"

Chadwick nodded.

"Okay. I feel like taking a ride. Tell your chauffeur to drive to Crown Beach, and stop in front of the Post Office. It's nearly twelve. I told the boy I would contact him either at noon or six at night. I imagine he's been waiting for me every day since he left."

THE END